GUILTY PLEASURE

SUZANA THOMPSON

❀ Created with Vellum

CHAPTER 1

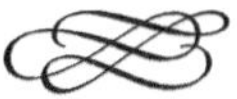

"You're a cold bitch," Dominic said with seething anger.

"You're a heartless bastard," Kendra shot back.

This type of exchange had been par for the course since Dominic had set his sights on seducing her at the beginning of the last school year, and she had repeatedly rejected him. She wasn't the only girl who had ever rejected him, but she was the only one who hadn't eventually caved to his seduction. He had put on the charm at first, using his smooth as silk moves on her as he tempted her with the thrill of having all of his attention focused on her.

She had seen him play this game before, though, and she knew that he was always the winner. He would come on all hot and bothered until he got what he wanted. It amazed her that girls continued to fall prey to his charms even though his reputation was well known.

Once he realized that she wasn't responding to any of his tricks, he had showed her the ugly person she had always known was lurking beneath that gorgeous face and fantastic body. He seemed to make it his mission to annoy her for the rest of the year. Her hope that he had forgotten about her over the summer had ended as soon as she saw the vicious glint in his eyes when he spotted her in the hallway.

He had sauntered up to her with an obnoxious smirk on his perfect face and leaned his six-foot frame over her as she tried to ignore him while testing out the combination on her new locker. "Kendra, my love, how was your summer? Did you miss me?"

"Like a bad case of syphilis," she responded in an offhand manner.

He laughed. "Such an old-fashioned girl. You're so quaint. That's why I like you."

"You don't like anyone except yourself," she said in the same bored tone.

"Kendra, you wound me. You really do." He gently took hold of her hand. "Why don't we start over? You know that I'm into you."

His falsely caring voice was already grating on her nerves, but his touch was what really got to her. "Cut the crap," she hissed and yanked her hand out of his grasp.

"Kendra," he continued in his smooth voice. "You're all grown up now. Don't you want to know what it feels like to be a real woman?"

She didn't take the bait and lecture him about how a woman was more than body parts. He had goaded her into enough rants last year that she knew he just enjoyed getting her riled up. Looking straight into his midnight eyes, she spoke slowly and clearly. "I'm not interested in you."

The friendly mask had slipped from his face, and he had lashed out at her with the bitch comment. He hadn't taken three steps away from her before a flirty girl in a miniskirt had flounced into his path. "Dominic! How was your summer?"

He whistled at her. "Lisa, you're looking good!"

She flushed with pleasure at his compliment. "Thank you."

Kendra's heart sank as Dominic walked off with Lisa. She was a nice girl, and he would break her heart. Kendra guessed that Lisa had lost about twenty pounds over the summer. Her new-found confidence was wasted on Dominic, who would use her and discard her just like every other girl he got into his bed. She hoped that Lisa would hold off on sleeping with him and come to her senses, but the way she had approached him didn't bode well.

Kendra was glad that this was her senior year of high school. She fervently hoped that she would never see Dominic again after graduation. Not only was it depressing to watch him cut a path of destruction through the hearts of the female population, but he was also an academic threat. Her relief was immense last year when the principal announced that there would no longer be a valedictorian beginning the following year. They were changing to the system used by colleges which distinguished students with Cum Laude, Magna Cum Laude, and Summa Cum Laude.

Kendra no longer had to worry about the humiliation of being academically bested by that oversexed jerk. How he found time to study in addition to his "extra-curricular" activities was beyond her. His intelligence was just one more thing on the list of unfair advantages bestowed upon an undeserving person. She could more easily dismiss him as a loser living out his glory days if he was stupid. Kendra could have at least consoled herself with the thought that his looks would eventually fade. It wasn't fair that such a despicable person might actually have a brilliant future ahead of him.

Her day improved tremendously when she discovered that he wasn't in any of her classes. She wouldn't have to suffer through another nightmare like last year when he was her partner in Chemistry. He wasn't even in the same lunch period with her. Now she would only have to deal with him for short periods of time when they happened to pass in the hallway. Or when he decided to seek her out by her locker before or after school, she amended. That wasn't a consideration today, because she had no reason to stop by her locker at the end of the first day of school.

She was walking toward the exit with her best friend when Dominic fell into step beside Caroline. Kendra continued what she was telling her about the field trip to France at the end of the year.

"That sounds like fun," Dominic commented. "I'm taking Chinese myself. It's more useful in the business world."

"Why'd you quit Spanish?" Caroline asked. She glanced nervously at Kendra, knowing that she frowned on engaging him in conversation.

"I didn't. I already got a decent base in it the first year, so I continued studying it on my own at home," he explained. "Chinese is much more difficult to master."

Caroline grimaced. "I couldn't deal with that. It's too hard."

"Just because something's hard doesn't mean that you should give up on it." His eyes were on Kendra as he spoke, but he didn't address her directly for once.

"I know," Caroline agreed. "I'm just starting to get burned out on school. You know?"

"Yeah, but you can't slack off until you get your college acceptance letter," he advised her.

This was why he was such a heartbreaker, Kendra thought. He could act like a decent person when he wanted to and have a normal conversation. She was grateful that he had spared Caroline from his advances. He was always uncharacteristically polite and respectful toward her. Dominic stepped aside as Adam walked up to put an arm around Caroline. She looked back apologetically at Kendra as her boyfriend talked nonstop while walking her toward his car. Kendra smiled and waved at her.

Her smile faded when Dominic followed her to her car. She ignored him as she clicked open the lock.

He stepped closer to her and spoke low in her ear. "I don't know why I feel this way about him when I know what he is, but it's only my body that wants him."

Kendra froze in shock at hearing those words come out of his mouth. It was impossible! That was from her private diary, and it was at home in her desk. There was no way he could have read it. Yet what he said next proved without a doubt that he had.

"I undress for him while he watches me the entire time with his midnight eyes. Then he starts to—"

"Stop!" Kendra pleaded.

"But I was just getting to the good part," he breathed in her ear.

She stepped away from him and tried to steady her breathing as she desperately thought of a way to salvage her dignity. First, she had to find out what had happened. "How did you—"

"Your sister gave it to me," he informed her.

Kendra gaped at him. Veronica! She was going to kill Veronica!

"I don't think she knew what it was," he defended her. "She's a sweet girl, but she's not the sharpest tool in the shed. I asked her for a piece of paper, and she gave me the entire notebook. Helpful girl that she is."

Even as she was reeling from this betrayal, she wondered which class Veronica could possibly have with Dominic. He was in advanced classes, and her sister certainly wasn't. It had to be study hall.

"Pop Culture," he supplied as if reading her thoughts.

It was a fun elective class, which was the only kind her sister would enjoy taking. The information he had provided gave Kendra an idea. "Wow, I can't believe she gave you her diary."

"Nice try, but Veronica wouldn't use words like smoldering or insatiable. Thanks for that, by the way. Also, you attributed your sex dream about me to subconsciously hearing the sounds of Veronica and her boyfriend fucking in the next room." He said all of that in the most matter-of-fact tone of voice imaginable.

It gave Veronica a sliver of hope that he would be reasonable. "Please give it back to me." Despite her humiliation, she kept eye contact with him and spoke in a strong, steady voice. He would use any sign of weakness against her.

"I will after you do what we both know you want to do."

He made no move to touch her, but she was trapped by his dark eyes. "I'm not going to have sex with you," she told him in a less steady voice.

"You finally admitted that it's what you want. Was that so hard?" His tone was ever so reasonable. It hid so well the monster underneath.

"I said that I'm not going to—"

He cut her off in a haughty manner. "Then I'm not giving you your diary back."

"You can't keep it," she protested, even though she knew it was useless to argue.

"It'll provide great masturbation material until you change your mind. I have to tell you; I'm impressed by what I've read so far. I had no idea that you have such a dirty mind. I guess it's true what they say. It's always the quiet ones."

Instead of his normal infuriating smirk, a slow, sensual smile played over his lips. "I take back what I said. You're not cold at all."

"You're still a heartless bastard," Kendra spat at him while she struggled not to cry from frustration.

"Actually, it was sexy bastard, as I recall." With that, his cocky smirk reappeared, and he walked away and left her to have a meltdown in her car.

CHAPTER 2

Kendra couldn't concentrate on anything as she waited for Veronica to get home from her boyfriend's house. She couldn't believe that her sister would do this to her. How many times had she covered for Veronica with their parents so she could hook up with her boyfriend? Such an act of betrayal was unprecedented between them, even though they were hardly close. They were simply too different to be friends as well as sisters.

Kendra was well aware that Veronica was considered the hot one. She had gotten their mother's blonde hair and blue eyes, while Kendra had their father's brown hair and brown eyes. Veronica was outgoing and popular, and she had been dating since the age of fifteen. Kendra didn't know why Dominic had fixated on her instead of her sister. Veronica was only sixteen, but that had never stopped him before. That, however, would probably have to change. If he wasn't eighteen already, he would be soon, so he would now have to watch the ages of the girls he took to bed.

She heard a car pull into the driveway and looked out to see that Veronica's boyfriend was dropping her off. Kendra was waiting for her when she walked inside the house. "My diary," she screamed. "You gave him my diary!"

Veronica looked bewildered. "What?"

Maybe the bastard was lying. She took a deep breath and tried to control herself. "Did you or did you not give Dominic Miller my diary?"

"You have a diary?" Veronica asked before an expression of comprehension finally showed on her face. "You mean that notebook I gave him?"

"Yes," Kendra ground out through gritted teeth. "Mine. Why did you have it?"

"Oh," she said. "I forgot to buy paper, so I borrowed yours."

Meaning, she hadn't bothered to get any school supplies but decided at the last minute that she might need to write something down on the first day of school—like a cute guy's number. Her cell phone had already been confiscated by teachers in the past, so she was laying low to make a good impression with her new teachers. Kendra wanted to scream in frustration again. "I had loose paper in my desk drawer. Why'd you take my notebook?"

"It's easier than carrying a folder. You know, in case I drop it or something. I figured you wouldn't mind, because there were only a few blank pages left, and you were probably gonna throw it away anyway." Veronica shrugged. "Turns out that I didn't even need it."

"Do you know what you've done?" Kendra demanded.

"I'll get you a new one," Veronica promised.

"It was my diary!" Kendra exploded. "You can't replace it."

"I'm sorry. I didn't know. Who writes in a diary anyway? What are you, twelve years old?"

Typical, Kendra thought. Veronica apologized in one breath and insulted her in the next. She didn't even realize that her carelessness had wreaked havoc on her sister's life. "Why would you give Dominic the whole notebook when he only asked you for one sheet of paper?"

Of course, she knew why. Veronica had a not-so-subtle crush on him.

She shook her head. "He did not. He asked me if I needed the notebook. I said no, so he asked if he could have it. I told him it had a bunch of writing in it, but he said that was okay. He only needed to show his next teacher that he had a notebook with him."

"A bunch of writing," Kendra repeated. "You didn't even bother to see what it was before you handed it over. Now he has my diary."

Veronica rolled her eyes. "I bet it's really exciting too. Dear diary, today I did homework. Then I did more homework. Then I studied to change it up a little."

Her sister didn't know anything about her secret life. Nobody did, and that was the point. Kendra was secretive about her desires. She was so ashamed of them that she couldn't even bring herself to share them with her best friend. That was why she had kept a diary to unburden herself in private. Her lust was a shameful secret, just like Hester's in the Scarlet Letter. In fact, she had even written Hester's name on the cover to remind her of how wrong her desire was, of how destructive it could be if she gave it free reign.

Kendra suddenly realized what had happened. "Does Dominic sit near you in Pop Culture?"

"Yeah, he sat right next to me today." Veronica confirmed her suspicion.

Of course, Dominic didn't need a notebook, because he was always academically prepared. He had asked Veronica for the notebook only out of curiosity as to why Hester was written on the cover. Kendra hid her face in her hands and wished that she could erase the entire day. Unfortunately, this was just the beginning. Things were only going to get worse. She wanted to disappear when she thought about everything she had written in that diary. He would know everything after he finished reading it, absolutely everything.

"Hey." Veronica finally showed some concern. "Are you okay?"

She looked at her clueless sister and sighed wearily. "Just don't touch anymore of my stuff without asking."

"Yeah," Veronica agreed. "I promise."

Kendra's stomach was so tied up in knots that she skipped dinner that evening and breakfast the next morning. She considered staying home from school but decided that she didn't want Dominic to think she was hiding from him. This wasn't going to go away, and she had to face it. Her resolve to ignore her desire for him hadn't changed. The only difference was that he now knew about it. He was going to be even more obnoxious than usual, but she would deal with it.

She still had to fight the urge to run away when she saw him. His eyes, however, were focused beyond her as he strode down the hallway with his mouth set in an angry line.

"You son of a bitch!" he yelled. "I'll fucking kill you!"

Kendra moved out of his path in fear, but he didn't spare her a glance as he came charging past her to punch Caleb Phelps. Several teachers hurried out of their classrooms to see what all the commotion was about as the two boys fought.

"What the fuck is your problem?" Caleb shouted after they were pulled apart by two male teachers.

"You're my fucking problem." Dominic's face was contorted in rage.

They were led away in opposite directions, but Kendra continued to stare after Dominic.

"What was that all about?" Caroline wondered.

"I don't know," Kendra lied.

She suspected that it was about what Dominic had read in her diary, but she had never expected him to react in such a way. He wasn't known for starting fights. He'd had to defend himself a few times against jealous boyfriends, but he had never before been the aggressor. Kendra couldn't understand why he had attacked Caleb. He couldn't possibly be jealous, could he?

CHAPTER 3

"Sorry, I can't chat. I have to go to detention."

Kendra had been about to open her locker when she heard Dominic speak. She turned around to look at him, curious to see the expression on his face after the rage he had directed at Caleb. His breezy, casual acknowledgement had revealed nothing about his state of mind.

He seemed just as intent on gauging her reaction as she was on reading him, because his dark eyes studied her without giving away his own emotions. "Did you hear?"

"I saw," she told him. "I was there this morning."

He appeared to be startled by this information. "Guess I was too distracted to notice."

"Why," she began to ask.

"I have to go. I'll call you later."

His long legs had already taken him around the corner and out of her sight before the meaning of his words dawned on her. How could he call her when he didn't have her number? In the next instant she realized how he had gotten it. Veronica again! Once Dominic called her, she would have his number and be able to block it, but she was still annoyed with her sister for not having any respect for her privacy.

"I thought you'd be happy," she said when Kendra confronted her. "He's the hottest guy at school."

"He's the sleaziest guy at school," Kendra retorted.

"You're so lucky," Veronica sighed. "I would drop Tyler in a minute if Dominic wanted me."

Kendra was disappointed but not surprised to hear her sister voice that sentiment. "Dominic would drop you five seconds after he got into your pants."

"It would be worth it. I heard he gives the best sex ever," Veronica told her.

Thinking about, or more specifically writing about, what kind of sex he gave was what had gotten her into this mess in the first place. "Please don't give Dominic anything else that's mine. Not ever!"

"Okay. Go ahead and become a lonely cat lady."

"I'm seventeen," Kendra exclaimed.

"Yeah, but if you won't even go out with the hottest guy at school, then what other guy is gonna have a chance?" Veronica asked.

"There is life after high school, you know." Kendra was thinking about the other guy she had taken a chance on. She had hoped that dating him would make her stop fantasizing about Dominic, but it hadn't worked. Caleb had never been able to replace Dominic in her fantasies. She wondered if that was why he had dumped her, because he had somehow sensed that she wasn't as into him as she should have been.

Dominic called her at eight o'clock that evening. "Hello, Kendra. How are you?"

"I was fine before you bothered me." She didn't know why she hadn't just hung up on him.

"Yes, I know how hot and bothered I make you."

She cursed herself for not watching what she said to him. Yet it would make no difference even if she said nothing. He already knew all her innermost thoughts about him. It gave her a strange contradictory feeling to think about him reading those words. Now that she had gotten over the initial shock and embarrassment, there was a sinfully erotic element to it. It somehow felt even more intimate than what she had shared with Caleb.

"Does it turn you on? Me reading your diary," he asked as if he could now read her mind as well. "You know, I've never been into porn. The real thing is so much more exciting. But reading your sexy thoughts has been a huge turn on for me."

She sat listening to him with the phone pressed to her ear as the things he was saying to her worked a seductive spell on her that made her forget her resolve to hang up on him.

"Pick any one of these fantasies, Kendra, and I'll make it a reality for you."

None of this was turning out the way she had expected it to when she discovered he had her diary. She had thought that he would mock her and humiliate her with her own words. He was supposed to make her hate him even more than she already did, not be making her desire for him increase by the minute. Well, she thought, nobody knows how to tempt you better than the devil.

"Why did you punch Caleb?" As curious as she was about the answer, the question was also an attempt to find her way out of the secret world into which Dominic had followed her.

"Caleb." There was a sharp edge to his voice when he said that name. "You really fell for his boy scout routine, didn't you? He played the perfect boyfriend until he got you into bed."

"You're one to talk," she snapped.

"Everybody knows my reputation. I don't pretend to be something I'm not so that I can seduce girls. They know what they're getting into with me. Caleb reels them in with romance, when all he wants is sex."

"That's not true," she said. "We had a relationship."

"Yes, the romance with the lifeguard that conveniently ends just before summer vacation does. That way he won't have to hold hands with you at school. Tell me, Kendra. If it was a relationship, why was the sex so crappy? He didn't even try to pleasure you."

She bristled at his criticism. "Maybe not everyone is such an expert like you."

"That's no excuse. There is plenty of information available about how to please a woman if he cared to learn, but he's only interested in pleasing himself. From what you wrote, his foreplay basically consisted of groping and clumsy fumbling."

It was surreal to be having this conversation with him. "What's it to you?"

"I have to admit that I wanted to be your first. I'm disappointed that you chose someone who doesn't even turn you on, when you want me so much," Dominic said.

"I did want him." Her voice sounded uncertain even to her ears.

"Really?" he questioned. "Is that why you continued to fantasize about me even after you started having sex with him?"

"This is crazy!" Kendra exploded. "You had no right to keep my diary. None of this is your business."

"It's all about your passion for me. What you were really thinking when you told me that you would never in a million years want me to touch you. How you imagined shoving me against the locker and kissing that smirk right off my lips. I urge you to go with that feeling the next time the mood strikes you."

Why couldn't he have a common name so he wouldn't know for sure that she was writing about him? "You've already read it, so may I have my diary back now?"

"You do know that we're not living in the days of the Scarlet Letter? You're not Hester, and there's no reason to be ashamed of your lust. It's a natural part of growing up."

She snorted. "So, I should just act on it. As long as it's with you," she added.

"I'm so disappointed," he read aloud. "I heard that the first time is not the best, but I thought it was supposed to be so much better after that. What a lie! Sex is so overrated."

"Stop doing that," she demanded. "It's bad enough that you read my diary. I don't need you to keep quoting from it."

"This should not be your experience of sex. Let me show you that sex is not overrated," he coaxed.

"That's generous of you," she said sarcastically. "But my answer is still no."

"Everything is out in the open now. You have no reason to fight your attraction to me," he argued.

"I have all the same reasons as before. You said yourself that everyone knows your reputation. I want more than that," she declared.

"Funny how you never mentioned that in your diary."

Then she did hang up on him, but she couldn't escape the truth of his words.

CHAPTER 4

Kendra saved Dominic's number into her contacts. She didn't know why. This secret connection they now had was weakening her resolve. He knew things about her that nobody else did. It was like he had glimpsed inside her mind, and there was something powerfully attractive about having him know her so intimately. The knowledge was there every time their eyes met. It created a heavy tension between them that was difficult to ignore. She was glad that he wasn't in her classes, because her thoughts strayed to him far too much as it was.

He called her every night, and she answered his calls. Sometimes they had normal conversations. "So, do you still want to go to law school?" Dominic asked.

That was another piece of information he had learned from her diary. "I'm considering it," Kendra said. "I'd like to help bring justice to victim's families."

"Corporate law pays the most," he told her. "You're going to have a lot of debt after law school."

"Money's not everything." Kendra was lying on her bed

talking to him in the dark. She liked being connected to him by the sound of his voice.

"I want to be rich," he stated.

She smiled to herself. "Why am I not surprised?"

"There's nothing wrong with being rich. It gives you the freedom to do what you want to do," Dominic said.

"You're definitely all about that," she responded dryly.

"I do what I want to do," he agreed. "Everyone has desires, but most people have to find excuses for doing what they want. They have to tell themselves they're in love, for example. I see something that I want, and I go after it. That's all the reason I need."

She disliked his view on life. "Just because you want something doesn't make it right."

"What about it is wrong? We're both single."

They were back to that again. He never ceased trying to seduce her. In the nearly three weeks since they began talking on the phone, he always managed to turn the conversation around to sex. He had declared that it was only fair that he share his fantasies with her too. She had threatened to hang up on him, but she had instead listened as he told her what he wanted to do to her. It was different than when she was alone fantasizing about him. Hearing him say such things aloud aroused her so much that she actually felt an ache between her legs where the blood had rushed to her nether parts.

"Have you ever thought about having me do that to you? You never wrote about it in your diary."

"No," she breathed.

"Did it make you wet? Thinking about feeling my tongue there."

She was too embarrassed to answer him, but he had guessed correctly. Her panties were definitely wet.

"I want to hear you come."

"What?" Kendra squeaked.

"It's called phone sex," he explained. "Play with yourself so I can hear you come."

"I'm not having any kind of sex with you," she said and hung up on him.

That had been yesterday, but he had been undeterred when he called her again today. "I'm coming to pick you up," he said now.

"You can't," she protested. "I'm in bed."

"At eight-thirty on a Saturday night? C'mon, Kendra. I want to see you. I still have another week of detention, so my time after school is limited. At least let me spend some time with you on the weekend."

"You got a month of detention?" Kendra asked. "That seems excessive."

"I was lucky not to get suspended. That would have hurt my chances of getting a scholarship. The counselor pleaded my case with the principal because of my academic performance. I told them that I lost my head over a girl, and I promised it would never happen again."

"Serves you right for stealing my diary," she huffed.

"I didn't steal it. It was given to me," he reminded her.

"Not by me. You still haven't given it back," she added.

"Come out with me, and maybe I will."

She rolled her eyes even though he couldn't see her.

"Please."

Don't do it, she told herself. "Okay."

Kendra changed out of her sweatpants and into jeans. It occurred to her that she had never told Dominic her address, but he found her house anyway. Fortunately, her parents had gone to see a movie, or she would have been forced to introduce him to them before she could go out with him. Veronica was out on a date with her boyfriend, so Kendra was home alone. She left a note for her parents saying that she was going out with a friend.

Dominic's arrival made her heart start pounding in anticipation. She had never been this nervous about her dates with Caleb, not even when she decided to have sex with him.

"Did you bring my diary?" Kendra asked after she opened the door.

He made a show of searching his pockets. "I must have left it at home."

He looked so temptingly good under her porch light that she couldn't even be mad at him. "Where are we going?"

"To my bedroom?" He shrugged at the look she gave him. "Can't blame me for trying."

Knowing that she was making a mistake, Kendra locked the front door and followed him to his car. "I'm surprised you don't have a date tonight."

She saw his smile before the interior lights went out. "I do."

This was definitely a mistake, she thought. "I told my parents I was going out with a friend. What'd you tell your parents?"

He pulled the car out onto the street. "My parents are divorced. I live with my dad."

"Oh. Did you get to choose who you wanted to live with?" She felt no qualms about asking him personal questions after he had invaded her privacy.

He laughed harshly. "No, I was only six when she left us."

"Divorcing your dad doesn't mean that she left you," Kendra assured him.

"It does. She found a boyfriend and decided that she didn't need the hassle of a kid anymore."

His bitter assertion distressed her. "Look," she said carefully. "I don't know what your dad told you, but sometimes when people get divorced—"

"My dad told me a bunch of crap about how she had to go take care of her sick parents. He always had an excuse about why she couldn't come home yet. I believed all of it until I realized that his sister was the one who had been sending me the birthday and Christmas cards that were supposedly from my mom. I thought that she was dead, but then I found the letters she had sent my dad asking him for money."

Kendra didn't know what to say. This kind of thing was beyond her experience. She knew a lot of kids with divorced parents, but not any who were abandoned by their mothers.

"He probably sent it to her too," Dominic continued in a derisive tone. "Do you want to know the best part? He has her as a friend on Facebook. He's on a date right now, but it doesn't matter. He'll never get over her."

"I'm sorry," Kendra said.

"Yeah, well, it's his problem." He lapsed into silence and turned on the radio after a few minutes.

He drove to the lake and parked the car. They sat looking at the moonlight reflecting on the water. "It's a beautiful night," Dominic said.

"Yeah," Kendra agreed.

The scene was very romantic, and Dominic's dark mood seemed to have dissipated. He reached out to touch her hand, which had been resting lightly in her lap. Her heartbeat accelerated at the contact while his thumb made lazy circles on her sensitive skin. All her nerve endings were alive with electric anticipation of more contact.

She turned her head to look at him, and her breath hitched as he leaned in toward her. The butterflies in her stomach fluttered frantically while his breath mingled with hers before he kissed her. Intense passion surged through her body and short-circuited her ability to reason. She ceased to think as primal instinct overwhelmed her. There was nothing else now except male and female.

When she finally came back to herself, she was on top of him in the driver's seat. He was lying all the way back in it with her body pressed against his, and his hands were gripping her ass while she kissed him hungrily. Kendra tore her mouth from his in shock. She didn't remember how she had gotten in this position, but she must have climbed over the seat at some point.

"Let go," she gasped.

He immediately did as she asked, but he groaned as she pushed herself up from him and awkwardly climbed back into the passenger seat. Her whole body was flooded with heat, and she was breathing heavily. It took a while before she could speak. "I want to go home."

"Give me a few minutes," he said with his eyes closed.

She had felt his erection when she had been lying on top of him, and she still felt an ache between her legs along with the discomfort of her wet panties. Kendra was glad that she wasn't wearing a skirt. She stared out at the lake and wondered what she was doing here with Dominic. What could she possibly expect to get out of this relationship? Was she that desperate for sex? She hadn't ever been before, so why was her desire for him so strong?

Dominic finally sat up and adjusted the seat so he could drive the car. They were silent on the way back to her house. "I'll call you tomorrow," he said as he pulled into her driveway.

"Goodnight," she said out of habit, and because she didn't know what else to say.

Surprisingly, he didn't mention their makeout session when he called her the next evening. They had the conversation that most people have before they start getting physical with each other. It was about their favorite movies and TV shows. What Kendra didn't realize until she thought about it much later was how adept he was at knowing just how far to push her. He would bring on the seduction then give her time to adjust to this new level of contact before trying to go further.

That Monday, however, she was at ease with him as he stopped to see her by her locker after school. Her stomach still did that fluttering thing when he approached her, but it was more controlled in this setting. She smiled at him.

"Dominic?"

His own smile faded as Lisa walked up to them.

"Dominic," she said again. "Can I talk to you?"

"I have to go to detention," he informed her curtly.

She seemed to wilt under his cold gaze. "Yeah, um, could I, could I call you later?"

"No. I've blocked your number."

Tears glittered in her eyes. "W-why?"

There was not a hint of emotion on his face. "I told you. It's over."

Lisa appeared to have forgotten that Kendra was even there. "I thought…I thought you liked me."

His smile froze Kendra's heart. "We had fun, didn't we?"

Lisa's face crumpled as the tears spilled from her eyes. She spun away from him and disappeared into the girls' bathroom. Dominic turned to see Kendra glaring at him. "What's wrong with you? How could you treat her that way? Can't you see that she's heartbroken?"

"She'll get over it," he replied without a shred of concern.

"God," Kendra exclaimed. "How could I forget what a heartless bastard you are?"

"Would you rather I screw both of you?"

Her eyes narrowed in anger. "You know what, Dominic? You can go fuck yourself."

"No need. There's always someone willing to do it for me. See you later sweetheart."

She wanted to strangle him as she watched him saunter casually down the hallway.

CHAPTER 5

*K*endra blocked Dominic's number, so she didn't know if he tried to call her. He kept his distance at school, but he watched her with his dark stare. Despite his silence, her attempts to ignore him were a failure. Now that she knew what it felt like to kiss him, her attraction to him was stronger than ever. She berated herself for having been stupid enough to let him touch her. There was no excuse for her behavior, because she had known what kind of guy he was.

She wasn't even upset for herself, since she had never expected anything more from him in the first place. It just infuriated her to watch him treat girls so callously and take whatever he wanted like it was his right to do so. Unfortunately, his smug reply was the truth. There was always somebody willing to give him what he wanted. She watched the girls flit around him like moths to the flame.

Since his detention ended, he had taken to standing a few feet away from Kendra's locker at the end of the day and watching her retrieve her backpack and whatever books she needed for homework. Right now, there was a redhead in a snug pair of jeans talking to him. Dominic's gaze kept flickering toward Kendra while the girl flirted with him. He seemed to have no trouble keeping up with the conversation, while Kendra was slow to respond to the boy who approached her.

"I'm sorry. What did you say?" Kendra asked.

Looking very nervous, Michael repeated the question. "Will you go to Homecoming with me?"

"Yes," she agreed decisively. "Yes, I will."

A delighted smile lit up his face. "Great! Um, okay, I'll see you tomorrow. Have a good evening."

"You too," she said as he hurried away after depleting all of his courage. Her heightened awareness of someone else set her on edge when she noticed him walking toward her.

"Don't you make a cute couple," Dominic said.

She instantly forgot her resolve not to talk to him. "What's it to you?"

"Just making an observation," he replied smoothly.

"I'm not interested in your observations," she snapped in irritation.

"No," he agreed with an insolent smirk. "That's not what you're interested in."

She knew what he was getting at, but she gazed coolly at him. "You're right. I'm interested in Michael."

"And here I didn't think you even knew his name. I'm impressed, Kendra."

Why the hell was he always leaning against somebody's locker like that, she wondered in annoyance. Was he always tired? Of course, he had read in her diary how sexy she thought his casual way of leaning was. It suddenly occurred to her that he might be doing it now to mock her. That thought raised her blood pressure, and it was her only excuse for the ridiculous words that flew out of her mouth. "Are you jealous?"

"Of Michael?" Actual mirth showed in his eyes. "He's a nice boy, but he's no competition for me."

She spoke the obvious. "Because you're not a nice boy."

"That's why you like me. Your thoughts about me aren't so nice, are they?"

He had peeled his body off of the locker he had been leaning against and stepped closer to her. Her traitorous body reacted to the seductive tone of his voice in ways she didn't want to think about. She was unable to think of a good comeback as she met his heated gaze. "He's the kind of guy I'm looking for."

"He's perfect for you," Dominic agreed to her surprise. "You can live out all of your prom queen fantasies with him."

Now he was definitely mocking her, and Kendra flushed under his knowing look. Damn him for keeping her diary! He knew that she had no such fantasies about prom. "Maybe I will," she declared defiantly.

"Be my guest," he offered agreeably. "Then when you get bored with him, you can live out your real fantasies with me."

Irked that what he had read in her diary made it impossible for her to deny her attraction to him, she tried to put a new spin on the situation. "Maybe my fantasies are about him now."

"They're not," he said with arrogant assurance. "You see, Kendra, you might think you're experienced, but you're really not. An attraction like ours doesn't happen every day. Don't get me wrong, I always enjoy sex. It's just much hotter with certain girls."

"We did not have sex," she hissed. "That kiss was a mistake, and it will never happen again."

"It was more than a kiss," he reminded her as his dark eyes burned with the memory. "It's like what we learned in Chemistry last year. Remember that combustion reactions are exothermic. That's what we are, Kendra. We produce our own heat."

"Stop lecturing me about chemistry. You drove me out there and tried to take advantage of me," she accused even as desire flared within her at the memory of his touch.

"Who was on top, Kendra?" Dominic asked. "The only thing I took advantage of was the reclining feature of my seat."

To her shame, Kendra felt herself becoming aroused as his words made her recall the sensation of straddling him in his car. "You're hot," she admitted. "Is that what you need to hear, you narcissistic jerk?"

"I already knew that," he said without a trace of humility. "What I didn't know is how hot *you* really are. It's one thing to write down your fantasies on paper, but it's another to be able to let yourself go like that in reality. Even most bad girls don't have that kind of passion. There's nothing hotter than finding a good girl with a wild side."

She chided herself for the rush she got at hearing him call her hot. How many times had she heard him compliment other girls? This was just another one of his tricks, and she wasn't falling for it. "It will never happen again," she repeated.

"It already has," he answered mysteriously, watching her with his midnight eyes. "We just haven't done it yet."

She was left to ponder the meaning of his words well into the evening before she realized that this was yet another one of his tricks to keep her thinking about him. As if she already didn't think about him enough. He probably hadn't spared her another thought after their conversation. She wondered what he was doing now. Maybe he was already hooking up with the redhead. Kendra asked herself why she was even thinking about that in the first place. She finally remembered that Michael had asked her to Homecoming. He was in her Calculus class, and even Dominic had called him a nice guy.

Banishing Dominic from her thoughts, she realized that this was the kind of news she was supposed to share with her best friend. In one of those odd coincidences, Caroline called her just as she picked up her cell phone.

"Can you talk?" Caroline asked.

Knowing that she was really asking if Kendra was sure that

nobody could hear their conversation, she answered that she was alone in her room. "What's up?"

"Today was our two-year anniversary."

Kendra knew that she was talking about her relationship with her boyfriend. Caroline and Adam were the only high school couple she knew that had been together that long. "Congratulations."

"Thanks. Everything is going great."

"That's good." Kendra wondered why this conversation required privacy.

"Lately I've been thinking about…"

She paused for a moment as Kendra waited patiently for her to continue. "Well, I'll be turning eighteen in a couple of weeks. Not that it's the reason I want to."

Kendra was beginning to get an inkling where Caroline was going with this, but she didn't interrupt.

"I know that he loves me, and I love him."

He had in fact told her that on their first anniversary. Kendra remembered that Caroline had been over the moon about it, because she had been afraid to tell him that she loved him until he told her first.

"It's just that now when we kiss, I always feel like I want more."

Kendra flashed back to kissing Dominic. She understood that feeling, but hers was caused by the wrong person. "Have you told Adam?"

"Yeah, and he says he'll wait for me, but I feel ready now."

Kendra thought back to the discussion she and Caroline had about sex back in ninth grade. They had agreed that it was okay if you loved someone. Kendra had never told her about having sex with Caleb. She only knew that they had dated over the summer. With a shock, Kendra realized that Dominic now knew her better than her best friend did.

She brought her mind back to Caroline's situation. "Okay, so what's the problem?"

"I'm scared," Caroline admitted.

Kendra cursed herself for her secrecy. Since Caroline didn't know that Kendra had already lost her virginity, she couldn't reveal to Caroline that it really wasn't that terrifying. "Tell him that," she advised. "He loves you, so I'm sure he'll do everything he can to make it easier for you."

"Yeah," Caroline agreed. "It's just fear of the unknown."

Kendra hadn't informed Caleb about her virginity, but she had insisted that he wear a condom. She had cried out in pain and then gritted her teeth until he finished.

"Was that your first time?" Caleb asked afterwards.

He seemed to take pride in it after she confirmed that it was. "You should get on the Pill. It feels much better without a condom."

Much better for whom, she had wondered but hadn't asked aloud. She certainly had no intention of getting a prescription just to please him. Kendra knew she had made a mistake when the sex didn't improve. She blamed it on not waiting until she was in love, like she had originally planned. Her curiosity about sex hadn't been a good enough reason to engage in it.

After her lousy experience with sex, she was surprised that she continued to have sexual fantasies about Dominic. He was probably all hype and would turn out to be just as big of a disappointment if she tried him out. She certainly wasn't in love with him. That was the one thing she was glad about out of this whole mess. At least he wouldn't be reading any lovesick thoughts about himself in her diary. On the other hand, that might have excused her fantasies about him.

After reassuring Caroline about Adam, Kendra told her about Michael asking her to Homecoming. Caroline was now excited about going shopping for dresses together. It was more excitement than Kendra could muster about her date with

Michael. He took her out for ice cream on Friday, and they got to know each other a little better.

Michael was sweet and considerate, and perfect for her in every way. He was intelligent and nice-looking with his warm brown eyes and friendly smile. They had a lot in common, because they were both in advanced classes and part of the same social circle. He even had a younger sister the same age as Veronica. Michael was exactly the kind of decent young man that she should be able to fall in love with. She could already tell that there would be no drama with him.

"Holding hands already?" Dominic commented on Monday. "You two better get a room. The sexual tension is overwhelming."

Kendra fixed him with an annoyed glare. "I'm sorry we're not living up to your high standards. Not everyone feels the need to make out in public."

Dominic grinned. "It's not my fault that the girl can't keep her hands off me. I wasn't trying to make you jealous."

"Don't flatter yourself. I couldn't care less what you do." She turned dismissively away from him to open her locker and gasped when his hands snaked past her waist to work the combination. She was now trapped between his arms as he stood behind her.

Unerringly turning to all the correct numbers of her combination, he unlocked the door and pulled it ajar. Then he leaned down to place his mouth next to her ear. "I saw them in the bathroom. His shirt lifted up when he was pulling her shirt off. I can't stop thinking about his abs and wanting to touch them."

"That was the first time I noticed you," he continued as Kendra struggled to breathe. "Do you remember how our eyes locked before you ran out? Megan never even knew that you were there."

"What's going on?"

Kendra's knees were so weak that it was a wonder she

managed to remain standing when Dominic stepped away from her to speak to the redhead. "Just helping the lady open her locker."

"It was stuck," Kendra found herself lying as she turned toward them. She sounded decidedly out of breath.

"You just have to give it a good yank," Dominic said as he put his arm around the redhead. A smile played over his lips as he watched Kendra try to compose herself.

The girl giggled. "That works for a lot of things."

"Thanks," Kendra mumbled and turned back to her locker.

"It was my pleasure," Dominic said as he walked away with the girl.

Kendra hoped their story had averted whatever gossip anybody who saw them just now was about to spread. It dismayed her that Dominic knew the combination to her locker. How had he found that out? Veronica didn't know it, so she couldn't be the culprit this time. Even more distressing was the fact that he seemed to be studying her diary so much that he was able to quote from it at random. Did he really think that he was going to seduce her with her own words?

endra's lukewarm physical response to Michael didn't change even after he kissed her. She liked him well enough as a person, but the sexual attraction was missing for her. It was the opposite with Dominic. She didn't like him at all as a person, but her attraction to him was incredibly strong. She wondered what was wrong with her. How could she want somebody only for his body?

She felt even guiltier about her lack of morals when she listened to Caroline talk about Adam. Without going into too much detail, she blushingly told Kendra that their first time had been mostly wonderful. "There's some pain at the end," she revealed. "Other than that, it was amazing."

"I'm so happy for you," Kendra said sincerely.

Caroline hugged her. "It'll happen for you too. When you fall in love…"

Kendra smiled and nodded, but she didn't hear the rest of that sentence. She doubted that she would ever fall in love with anyone. Caroline seemed to have found everything she wanted in one person, whereas Kendra's mind and body seemed to want very different things. Maybe she was just one of those women who had terrible taste in men, in which case she should probably stop dating altogether.

Her relationship limbo continued, however, as Michael accompanied her to Caroline's eighteenth birthday party. She now felt stuck in the situation she had created by accepting a date with him as she and Caroline went shopping for Homecoming dresses. At least Dominic had stopped hanging around near her locker, so she didn't have to be confronted by the cause of her guilt every day. She naively thought that he was now going to leave her alone.

She found the first one on a Friday morning. It was a neatly folded piece of paper set on the top shelf of her locker. Kendra immediately suspected Dominic, because he knew the combination to her locker. She held the paper inside her locker and shielded it with her body before she opened it to find that it was actually two sheets of paper folded together. Even that precaution didn't seem like enough as she quickly glanced at them and folded them closed again to stuff inside her purse. Kendra put her backpack away and took out the books she needed. She closed her locker and turned to see Dominic watching her.

Her eyes blazed with anger as she marched up to him. "I'm sick of your games! Give it back to me."

His lazy smile did nothing to improve her temper. "I'm not finished editing it yet. I must say, though, that it has a lot of potential."

"Are you really that pathetic?" Kendra sneered at him. "Are you that desperate for me to stroke your ego?"

"That's not what you want to stroke. Is it, sweetheart?" His filthy suggestion was tempered by the soft, almost tender tone of his voice.

She glared at him and chose to comment on the last thing he had said. "Stop calling me that."

"What should I call you then? Sexy? Yeah, you are, but it doesn't seem like a good nickname for you. You've got that prickly exterior, but underneath you're sweet as honey." He dropped his volume even more as he stepped closer. "I bet you taste even sweeter."

Momentarily thrown by him reverting to the friendly, playful person he had been when he first began trying to seduce her at the beginning of the last school year, she stared into his magnetic dark eyes.

"Kendra," he coaxed in a seductive voice that was softer than velvet. "Take what you want."

In that moment, she wanted nothing more than to kiss him. His eyes began to smolder as her lips parted. The warning bell jarred her out of the spell he had cast, as Dominic swore angrily at the interruption. Shame flooded her cheeks with heat, and Kendra hurried away from him to her first period class.

She had almost done the unthinkable. Kissing him in public would have destroyed her reputation and her new relationship with Michael. She couldn't understand what had just happened. How had he managed to subvert her anger into a desire to throw caution to the wind and kiss him right there in the open?

And all of that after his latest mockery of her fantasies about him. She waited until lunch to go into a stall in the bathroom and read the papers he had left in her locker. The first was a photocopy of a page from her diary. She cringed at the description of one of her sex dreams about him. Worse still was the fact that he had added his own notes to enhance the erotic details of what he had done to her in the dream. If that wasn't bad enough, she actually became aroused while she read what he had written.

Kendra crumpled the papers and stuffed them back into her purse. She flushed the toilet in a paranoid attempt to cover her reason for being in the stall. There was nobody else in the bathroom as she stepped out of the stall and washed her hands. She splashed some water on her face to cool her heated cheeks.

"Where have you been?" Caroline asked when she finally sat down at their table.

"I had to stop in the bathroom," Kendra said.

Caroline studied her with concern. "Are you okay? You look kind of flushed. Maybe you should go have the nurse take your temperature."

"No, I'm fine." She knew perfectly well what had caused her spike in temperature, but she couldn't tell Caroline about it.

When had she started keeping so many secrets from her best friend? Kendra could only imagine Caroline's shocked reaction to the indecent things she had written in her diary about Dominic.

"Aren't you going to eat?" Caroline gestured to the empty space on the table in front of Kendra.

"I had a candy bar earlier," she lied. "It spoiled my appetite."

To her relief, Caroline accepted her answer and began to tell her about something funny that had happened in one of her classes. Kendra was able to take her mind off of the incident with Dominic until she saw him waiting by her locker after school. To add insult to injury, he unlocked it for her when he saw her approaching.

"Stay out of my locker," she demanded.

He stepped out of her way but remained hovering beside her. "I'm just concerned about you. Caroline was worried that you might be running a fever."

Damn! She had forgotten that Caroline had English class with him. She pointedly ignored him while she gathered her things.

Dominic waited until the students nearby walked away in boisterous excitement over the weekend. "So, it made you hot?"

Kendra refused to answer his question. "Where's your redhead? Did you dump her already?"

"It's your fault," he said. "Ever since that night at the lake, all I can think about is you."

"Yes," she agreed sarcastically. "After you had your way with her, all you could think about was me."

"That's why you're upset with me?" Dominic questioned her in surprise. "Because of some girl?"

"Some girl," Kendra repeated angrily. "Didn't you even bother to learn her name before you slept with her?"

"Why are you acting like a jealous girlfriend? I thought you and I understood each other." He reached out to touch her arm. "We want the same thing."

She shook him off, not sure if she was more disgusted with him or herself. "What I want is for you to give me my diary back and leave me alone. Stop trying to humiliate me."

"Humiliate you?" He looked genuinely taken aback. "How did I humiliate you? I've kept this our secret. I even folded the paper so no one could read it if they were with you when you opened your locker. I knew you'd be smart enough to figure out that it was from me."

Even under these odd circumstances, she couldn't help feeling flattered that he had called her smart. She had certainly never heard him use that compliment as a seduction technique before. "Speaking of that, how did you get my locker combination?"

"You were testing it out when I was talking to you on the first day of school," he reminded her.

"Oh, now I remember," she said with false sweetness. "It was when you called me a bitch."

"I apologized for that," he said impatiently. "Are you going to hold the past against me forever?"

"How about yesterday? In fact, how about today? You don't even have enough decency to return my personal property to me," she fumed.

His wicked expression appeared without warning. "I gave part of it back."

"That was only one page, and it was a copy," she exclaimed in frustration.

"Much improved, as I'm sure you agree."

That smile was her undoing. "You arrogant asshole," she yelled as she came at him.

She got in a few ineffectual hits before he caught her flailing arms. "You're even sexier when you're mad. So much passion." He leaned in to kiss her.

"Don't."

That one word stopped him instantly. His eyes were still burning into hers, but he let go of her. "Come over tonight. My dad's going out."

"I have a date with Michael." As she answered him, it occurred to Kendra that this entire conversation was crazy. Instead of going home like a normal person, she was caught up in arguing with Dominic. Her only saving grace was that no one was around to witness their exchange. The hallway emptied quickly on Friday afternoons.

"Why?" He stood there regarding her with a quizzical expression. "You're not even attracted to him, so why are you going out with him?"

"I like him. He's a good person, and we have a lot in common." She didn't know why she was explaining herself to him.

"So, it's a friendship," Dominic said.

"No," she denied. "It's romantic."

"Romantic, but not sexual."

Suddenly uncomfortable with how close they were standing, Kendra stepped back. "That's none of your business."

"I'm just trying to understand why you're dating someone who doesn't turn you on."

His dark eyes saw too much, and she looked away from him. "That takes time. Normal people don't just jump into bed."

"It doesn't take time. You're either attracted to someone or you're not," he insisted. "The only reason they don't jump into bed is because they're not acting on the attraction."

"That's not true," she cried. "A lot of people are friends first before they become romantically involved."

"Only because the attraction was there from the beginning, but they were denying their feelings," he said. "Just like you were denying your feelings for me."

She bristled at his constant reminders of his knowledge of her secret thoughts about him. "We were never friends."

"No, our attraction is too strong to be masked by friendship." His voice dropped dangerously low again. "We get hot just thinking about each other." He stepped forward into her personal space. "Wasn't that the cause of your fever today?"

Kendra shifted nervously away from him. "You can't write those disgusting things in my diary."

"I haven't written anything in your diary. I only made a few notes on the page I copied. You had a good start, but the finish left a lot to be desired. It's understandable, since you've never experienced great sex." His sensual smile promised such an experience. "Of course, I can rewrite them to your taste. Which part, exactly, did you find disgusting?"

"You're impossible," she declared in frustration. "I'm going home."

"Happy reading," he called after her with a smirk she didn't see, because her back was turned to him.

"I threw it away," she shot back without turning around.

"No, you didn't," he voiced aloud in too low of a volume to be heard by the retreating girl. Unbeknownst to him, his smile held genuine affection for her.

In her haste to leave, she had forgotten to take her things out of her locker. Dominic grabbed her backpack and closed her locker. They met up in the nearly empty parking lot. She had started walking back when she saw him bringing her backpack to her. Instead of thanking him, she took it from him and stormed off to her car without another word. He watched in amusement as she sped out of the parking lot.

Kendra slowed down as she left the school behind. For the thousandth time, she told herself that she couldn't allow Dominic to get to her like that. She just had to get through this year, and she would probably never see him again. Last year had been much tougher when she'd had to deal with him in class every day. Of course, he hadn't had her diary last year. He was obviously never going to give it back, so she had to let it go. She had been planning to burn the damn thing after this anyway.

She went straight up to her room when she arrived home. Then she took the paper out of her purse and sat down on her bed to read it again. This entry described her first sex dream about Dominic, and it was the passage he had started quoting to her on the first day of school when Veronica gave him her diary.

I am looking at myself in the mirror when I see Dominic standing behind me. Not turning around, I undress for him while he watches me the entire time with his midnight eyes. Then he starts walking toward me, keeping eye contact with me in the mirror. He wraps his arms around my waist before sliding one hand up to cup my breast as he kisses my neck.

Dominic had added a note here. *See next page.*

Kendra looked at the words he had written on the next page, and felt heat unfurl in her belly as she read them.

His thumb lightly brushes over my nipple, and I moan, wanting more contact. He holds me steady against him with his other arm wrapped firmly across my waist while he continues to tease me by grazing his thumb ever so lightly over my nipple.

Kendra had written that she then turned around and kissed him before he carried her to the bed. She described watching him undress and finally getting to touch his chiseled abs before he kissed her and thrust into her. Dominic had added another note here. *Not yet. See next page.*

After he drives me mad with desire, he slides his hand down between my legs as he kisses my neck. He begins to move his finger teasingly close to my clit, and I beg him to touch me. I moan as he strokes me and brings me closer to climax. It turns me on to see myself in the mirror while he touches me. He watches me come while he holds me against him.

To be continued...

Kendra folded the papers and set them at the bottom of her desk drawer with notebooks on top of them. Then she thought about how Veronica had taken her diary out of this same drawer, and she took them back out. Looking around her room, she decided to hide them in her underwear drawer. Nobody would look in there. She didn't want to think about why she was keeping such a thing.

CHAPTER 7

*D*ominic hadn't been lying when he said that he couldn't stop thinking about Kendra. True, that hadn't stopped him from hooking up with Danielle. Of course, he knew her name, but it was more fun to mess with Kendra than admit that. The redhead was sexy, but she didn't hold his interest the way Kendra did. He had never spent so much time trying to seduce a girl before. It had already been more than a year since Kendra had first spurned his advances.

In time, he had become frustrated with her rejection and endeavored merely to annoy her. He had succeeded spectacularly in that regard. It had satisfied his desire to get a reaction out of her. If he couldn't seduce her, he could at least piss her off.

When he first discovered that Veronica had given him Kendra's diary, he had thought it was a prank. He was sure that Kendra had written Hester on the cover to arouse his curiosity and instructed her sister to give it to him as a way to mock his failed seduction of her. Dominic suspected that she had amused herself over the summer by concocting this scheme to make fun of him. He decided to play along before revealing that she hadn't fooled him. Her shocked reaction, however, had convinced him that the diary was real.

After taking a more in-depth look at it, he understood why she was so easy to anger. She was angry with herself because of her attraction to him, and she was angry with him for being a constant source of temptation and frustration for her. Kendra fantasized almost as much about him as he did about her. Dominic was impressed by her restraint. If she had been coming onto him all the time, he wouldn't have been able to suppress his desire.

Her sex fantasies about him were extremely arousing for him to read about, but something else happened to him as well. So many of her private thoughts were about him that he subconsciously began to feel like she was his. That was why he became enraged when he read that Caleb had taken her virginity. Dominic had never experienced jealousy over a girl before. It was shockingly intense, and he now understood why people lost their cool over their lovers.

The irony was that Kendra wasn't even his lover. She was still fighting her desire for him, but he had renewed hope that she would eventually succumb to it. His idea to use her fantasies to his advantage seemed to be having an effect on her. She had almost allowed him to kiss her at school today.

He had originally planned to give her back her diary after he finished reading it. Yet he found himself inexplicably reluctant to part with it. He enjoyed the erotic content within, but it was more than that. Every time he opened it, he felt connected to Kendra. She had spent countless hours writing it by hand. As he read her secret thoughts, he felt closer to her than he had ever felt to any other girl.

Now that he was "editing" it, he was imagining her reading his thoughts too. He wanted to excite her and please her, and he put a lot of effort into trying to prove to her that he could make her fantasies even better if she would let him.

She had already proven to him that the reality of being with her was much better than he had imagined. The memory of making out with her in his car made him crazy with desire for her. He had kissed her, and she had responded with wild passion.

Dominic had never seen a girl overcome by desire so quickly. Even the girls who threw themselves at him didn't show that kind of abandon. Their seductions of him were calculated and choreographed to feature them at their sexiest. The way they moved and undressed revealed an awareness of showing off their bodies to their best advantage. Kendra, however, had been driven by pure lust as she climbed out of her seat to straddle him. She had kissed him with such hunger that he had moaned in pleasure. Seeing how hot she was for him was the most erotic thing he had ever experienced.

She had been so into it that he was amazed she had found the willpower to stop. He was so turned on that it had been a struggle not to stop her from climbing off his lap. Even now, the memory never failed to arouse him.

For the first time in his life, he was focusing on one girl to the exclusion of all the others. Several girls had approached him after he stopped seeing Danielle, but he had yet to choose his next sexual partner. More than anything, he wanted it to be Kendra.

Dominic perused her diary, looking for an entry he could make hotter. He needed something that he could make a reality for her, so that she might seriously consider it. There were lots of fantasies about having sex at school in empty classrooms. It made sense that she would daydream about him at school, since that was where she saw him. While it turned him on to imagine taking her on top of a desk, a girl like Kendra would never do something like that in a place where anybody could walk in on them.

He found one that she had written one weekend when she

was home alone. Apparently, Veronica sometimes entered beauty pageants. After many arguments, their parents had finally stopped forcing Kendra to attend them. Dominic smiled as he read how she had ignored the casserole her mother had left in the fridge for her and eaten potato chips for dinner and ice cream for breakfast. His amusement was replaced by lust as he read her fantasy about him.

The bathroom is steamy, because I forgot to turn on the fan before I took a long, hot shower. I am reaching for a towel when the door opens. Dominic walks in, and his dark eyes rake over my dripping wet body. I can't move, because I'm too weak with desire. He picks me up and kisses me while I wrap my legs around him. He takes me into the bedroom and drops me on the bed. I unzip his jeans, and he doesn't even pull them all the way down, because he can't wait to have me. He's thrusting into me and moaning.

Dominic noticed that she didn't seem to know much about foreplay, probably because that lousy fuck Caleb had deprived her of it. It irked him that she had turned to that fake for what Dominic could have done a much better job providing for her. Getting back into the proper frame of mind, he began to add his notes to her fantasy. They started right after the part where she was too weak to move.

He kneels down before me and starts to lick the drops of water off my breasts. His tongue swirls around one nipple, then the other. His hand is at the small of my back, supporting me while his tongue drives me crazy. He's sucking on my nipples now, alternating between breasts while my moans fill the bathroom.

Dominic then moved on to the part in the bedroom after he dropped her on the bed.

He kneels down on the floor, and his head dips between my legs to taste me. His tongue teases me, licking tantalizingly close to my clit. Then he begins to lick me there, and I moan as my orgasm builds. I shudder as I come on his tongue.

Dominic was so turned on by this fantasy that he decided to

go masturbate in the shower. He wondered if Kendra ever masturbated. If she did, she had never mentioned it in her diary. He would love to watch her pleasure herself. Basically, he would love to see her come. He wanted to hear the sounds she would make. It turned him on to think about her being turned on.

He got to school early on Monday so he could leave the description of her fantasy in her locker. This time she took it off the shelf and put it into her purse without reading it first. Her brown eyes met his as she turned around to look for him, but she didn't confront him.

As luck would have it, he was on a bathroom break during second period when he saw her walking out of the girls' restroom. Her curiosity must have made her too impatient to wait until lunch to read his notes. He could tell that she had read it, because her entire face flushed with heat when she saw him approaching her. Before he could say a word, she grabbed his arm and pulled him into the bathroom with her.

"Pick me up," she demanded and moved his hands to her waist.

Without a clue as to what was going on, he did as she asked. Kendra then wrapped her legs around his waist and grabbed hold of his neck to pull him into a ferocious kiss.

CHAPTER 8

Fever raged through her body as Dominic leaned her against the wall and tilted her hips. She could feel the unyielding hardness of him pressing into her core while his tongue did amazing things to her mouth. Kendra's grip on his shoulders tightened as the ache between her legs intensified.

The sound of her moan broke through her sensual haze and reminded her that someone might hear them. She turned her head to break the kiss, but he recaptured her lips.

"Stop," she gasped when she managed to tear her mouth from his again.

Dominic pulled back to stare at her, and the look in his dark eyes heated her blood until it flowed through her like liquid fire. He began to grind into her, and another moan escaped her.

"Let—oh!—let me down."

"You like that?" His desire-roughened voice sent even more heat flooding into her core.

Her fingers were digging into his shoulders now. "Let me down," she panted.

He stopped grinding but kept her pinned to the wall. "Gonna

make you come later." With that promise, he finally released her.

She stood catching her breath before turning on him. "Don't you ever touch me again!"

His sexual frustration quickly flared into anger at her attitude. "You're the one who dragged me in here, so don't fucking blame this on me."

She steamrolled right over that fact. "I just wanted a kiss, not to be fucked in the bathroom."

"Maybe if I did fuck you, you wouldn't be such a bitch," he lashed out at her.

Kendra sucked in a breath as her gaze hardened. "Really, Dominic? You're actually going to tell me that I need to get laid?"

"I think scratching that itch would do wonders for you," he said with insulting gall.

She looked at him with icy disdain before exiting the bathroom. Kendra scowled in annoyance over the slowly subsiding throbbing between her legs as she walked back to class. What she had done had been beyond stupid. All her dirty thoughts about him had finally led her astray. Why hadn't she thrown away those damned papers without reading them? She should have at least waited until she got home.

Her curiosity had made it difficult to focus on class, so she had decided to take a little peek after asking for a bathroom pass. She was going to just quickly skim through it and read it in more detail later. Instead, she got caught up in the erotic images created by his words. When she stepped out of the bathroom and saw the object of her desires himself, it had seemed like just another fantasy.

Her realization that it was really happening had failed to be the horrifying shock it should have been. She had wanted to finish what she had started, because it felt much better than any of her fantasies. Fortunately, she hadn't completely lost her mind yet, and common sense had somehow prevailed.

Dominic had showed his true colors once again. That was no surprise, but she kept having to be reminded of it for some inexplicable reason. He was what he was, and she had known that. It was her own behavior that was troubling her. She had thought that she knew herself better than that.

Kendra had done so well with controlling herself around him the entire last school year. He'd even been her partner in Chemistry, and he'd taken every opportunity to "accidentally" touch her or brush up against her. She remembered one particularly mortifying instance when she'd become lost in a fantasy of him knocking the test tubes off the table and having his way with her. Dominic had brought her out of it by snapping his fingers in front of her face. His smirk had made her feel like he could read her mind, which was completely ridiculous, but it had made her blush crimson.

Now he really did know what she had been thinking then, because she had written about it in her diary. She decided that her diary was what had kept her from acting on her desires, since it had been an outlet for her feelings about him. Without it, her pent-up passion was spilling over into real life. She could just start another diary, but she was loathe to do so after what had happened with her other one.

"Not hungry again?" Caroline asked.

Kendra looked at her best friend and made a decision. "I'm upset."

The instant concern on Caroline's face made Kendra feel like an idiot for being so secretive. "What happened?"

"Not here," Kendra said. "Call me after Adam drops you off."

"How about I ride home with you?" Caroline offered. "We can hang out at my house for a while."

Kendra smiled gratefully. "Thanks." Of course, her friend was always there for her, if only she would let her be.

She would have more drama to deal with before the day was over, but she was hoping that seeing Dominic again wouldn't be part of it. He, however, relished being the bane of her existence, so he was waiting beside her locker after school.

"Don't you ever go to your own locker?" Kendra snapped at him.

"I was thinking we could share yours," he replied with casual ease.

She glared at him. He really was unbelievable to come here and act like he hadn't been a prick to her this morning. "I don't want to share anything with you."

"We're back to that, are we sweetheart? Why do you continue this pretense when we both know the truth? You want to share much more than a locker with me."

His silky voice seemed to thrum through her blood, reminding her uncomfortably of being draped over his hard body earlier in the day. "Caroline," she called in relief.

"Adam's gonna get my stuff and bring it over later," she explained as she hurried toward them. "Hi, Dominic."

His entire demeanor changed at her approach. "Hi, Caroline." Even the way he smiled at her was different than the way he smiled at Kendra. He looked about as dangerous as a lamb whenever Caroline was around.

She should just keep Caroline by her side at all times, and he would cease to be a threat, Kendra thought in bemusement as she grabbed her things out of her locker.

"Well, I'll see you ladies tomorrow," Dominic said amiably. "Think it over and let me know."

"Let you know what?" Caroline asked.

"Kendra and I were discussing the merits of sharing a locker," he said with a straight face.

Kendra's hand itched to slap him. His smile was just on this side of decent as he saw her eyes flash with anger. "I think I was clear about my answer."

"Yes," he agreed. "You were very direct. I appreciate naked honesty."

"Um, okay," Caroline said in confusion as she saw the murderous look in Kendra's eyes. "See you tomorrow."

Kendra looked straight ahead as she stalked past Dominic. That insufferable jerk had to taunt her with thinly veiled references to their makeout session. He wasn't ever going to let her forget about it. How was she going to get through the rest of this year, when she had already thrown herself at him at school of all places?

"What's wrong?" Caroline asked as soon as they were seated in Kendra's car.

"I kissed Dominic," Kendra blurted. She had planned to work her way up to revealing this, but it was out now.

The shock she had expected was absent from Caroline's face. "It finally happened."

Kendra was somewhat offended by this reaction. "What do you mean finally?"

"The tension between you guys has been so thick that it was only a matter of time."

"That's such a cliché." Kendra turned the key in the ignition and pulled out of her parking space.

"There's a reason things become cliché," Caroline reasoned. "It's because they're pretty common. Anyway, what are you upset about?"

Kendra glanced at her incredulously. "I just told you. I kissed Dominic."

Caroline exhaled in obvious relief. "You had me worried. I thought something was really wrong."

"Something *is* really wrong. Something is really wrong with *me*," Kendra clarified. "How could I do that? I know what kind of guy he is."

"A really gorgeous guy," she enthused. "What?" Caroline

asked after Kendra shot her a look. "I have eyes, and he's extremely easy on them."

"Caroline!" Kendra exclaimed.

She shrugged. "There's nothing wrong with looking."

"Yeah," Kendra agreed. "The problem is that I did more than look."

Caroline sobered and sympathized with her. "It's a problem because of Michael."

"God, Michael!" Kendra cried in anguish. "I didn't even think about him."

"What are you going to do?" Caroline now realized the dilemma her friend was in.

"We're going to break up. I cheated on him. I never thought I'd be a cheater," she ended sadly.

"You've liked Dominic a lot longer," Caroline consoled her. "If only you knew that he liked you back, you wouldn't have started dating Michael."

"The only person Dominic likes is himself! All he does is use girls."

Kendra's outburst startled Caroline. "But I thought you guys—"

"It's all physical," Kendra cut her off impatiently. "I mean, that's what he's known for, so what else could it be?"

"Maybe," Caroline began.

"There is no maybe about it. I'm not going to delude myself the way all those other girls did."

Her tone of voice was so harsh that Caroline was afraid to upset her further by asking too many questions. She would let Kendra tell her at her own pace. Despite his reputation, Caroline liked Dominic. He had always been nice to her, and he had a lot of good qualities. She had always believed that all he needed was to find the right woman. Kendra obviously didn't share that opinion.

Caroline's parents weren't home from work yet, so they had

privacy to talk. "How's everything going with you and Adam?" Kendra asked as she stared out the living room window.

"Better than ever," Caroline replied with a blush Kendra didn't see. She would have been alone with him right now if it hadn't been for her friend's crisis.

"I'm sorry I'm cutting into your alone time," Kendra said as if reading her mind.

"Don't be silly. I always have time for you. Come and sit down," she urged.

Kendra sighed and walked over to sit down beside Caroline. "I don't even know where to begin."

"You and Dominic," Caroline suggested. "How did it happen?"

Kendra leaned back and stared at the ceiling. "Well first of all, he has my diary."

Caroline's mouth dropped open in surprise. "He was in your room?" She knew that Kendra would never take her diary to a public place.

"No, my wonderful sister gave it to him. Before you ask, she didn't know it was my diary. Not that it excuses her taking my things without asking. Anyway, I wrote some stuff in there about him, and now he knows I find him attractive," Kendra explained.

"That must have been embarrassing, but it's not like you're the only girl who's fantasized about kissing him," Caroline said.

Kendra sat up and looked directly at Caroline. "The fantasies I wrote about involved a lot more than kissing."

Her eyes widened as she realized what Kendra meant. "Oh."

"Now he thinks that he can take advantage of me because of it, but I'm not going to let him win," she declared defiantly.

"Is he blackmailing you?" Caroline asked in a horrified whisper.

"No," Kendra admitted. "He's just, well he's…"

She felt the color creeping into her cheeks. "I kissed him, but it can't happen again."

Caroline hid her smile as Kendra stood up and began to pace back and forth. "Why not?"

Because he's too damn good at it, Kendra thought. Because next time I might not be able to stop. "Because it can't," she repeated. "I know you've got some kind of blind spot where he's concerned, but he is not boyfriend material."

She sighed deeply. "Thanks for listening, but now I've got to go break up with a nice guy because of that jerk."

Caroline walked her to the door. "Call me later."

Kendra texted Michael after she sat down in her car. He replied that she was welcome to come over. His delight over her unexpected visit faded quickly as she confessed that she had cheated on him. He asked to know the name of the boy, but she wouldn't tell him. Michael said that they could work it out if she came clean about the whole thing, but that he would never be able to trust her if she kept the guy's identity a secret. Shaking her head sadly, she told him that she was sorry and left his house.

As she drove away, she thought that she couldn't even trust herself. How could she expect anyone else to trust her? She was tainted by her sordid association with Dominic.

CHAPTER 9

She was driving him crazy.

Dominic replayed the scene in the bathroom as he masturbated for the second time that night to the same memory. He had felt her passion when she kissed him in his car, but he hadn't been able to see her that clearly in the moonlit darkness. During their makeout session this morning, she had attacked him with the same feral lust. The difference was that it was plainly visible on her face when she told him to stop. He had looked into her eyes and seen how turned on she was, and he knew that he had done that to her. His reserved, proper Kendra was moaning and panting with every thrust of his erection against her core. He was so fucking hot for her that he was about to break his own rule about not having sex at school.

Dominic was always the one in control. He liked to tease girls and get them all hot and bothered. The ones who were willing to engage in foreplay at school were left aroused and waiting for him to finish the job. He would then meet them after school and find them wet and ready. His ability to seduce girls with his sexy games was part of the reason he got so much action. The pattern was predictable and sexually satisfying to him.

Kendra ran so hot and cold that he couldn't get a handle on her. Many girls had aroused his lust, but no one else had such a volatile effect on him. Just when he thought it was a sure thing, she'd give him the cold shoulder. It was maddening, because she always flipped on him right after making him wild with desire for her. He was usually a smooth operator, but she provoked him into speaking without thinking.

Kendra's behavior was not predictable. He had never expected her to initiate anything sexual with him at school. Dominic remembered that she had also surprised him after she had caught him in the bathroom with Megan. He had expected to hear all kinds of rumors about them having sex at school, but she hadn't said a word to anyone. After reading her diary, he knew that she hadn't even told Caroline about it.

Dominic had lied when he said that was the first time he had noticed Kendra. He had actually noticed her the previous year before that incident when they were in tenth grade. Caroline— or rather her breasts—had caught his interest first. They were worthy of a Playboy centerfold, but she must have been self-conscious about them. She took every opportunity to cover them up instead of showing them off. That was a little difficult to do in gym class, however, and Dominic was able to ogle them discreetly. He had decided to approach her at lunch in the hope that it wouldn't be so obvious that her body was what had attracted him to her.

"You're a beautiful boy, Dominic Miller, but I'm in love with someone else," she had told him with the most open, honest expression he had ever seen on any girl's face.

Dominic had been charmed by her sweet nature and lack of pretense. "Lucky him."

"Oh, he doesn't know yet," Caroline revealed. "I'm waiting for him to notice me."

"Why don't you tell him that you like him?" Dominic suggested.

"Because I want him to notice me on his own. If it's true love, it's meant to happen. Fate will bring us together," she explained with romantic, girlish illusion.

Dominic was a realist who didn't believe in fate. If you didn't go after what you wanted, you might never get it. "Are you sure this guy deserves you? He must be pretty dense if he hasn't noticed your crush on him."

An amused smile played over her lips. "So, you always notice when a girl has a crush on you?"

"And exploit it, as I'm sure you've heard. I'm kind of an expert at reading women," he bragged.

"Really?" Caroline asked in a coy voice that he already knew wasn't suited to her nature. "Interesting."

Her eyes flitted away for just an instant, but he caught the movement. Her smile was genuine as she looked at him. "I have to go cheat on my diet now. See you later, beautiful boy."

"See you later, Caroline." His eyes followed the direction she took, but he wasn't looking at her.

He was watching the brunette she had inadvertently glanced at when she had questioned his boasting about reading women. The girl suddenly noticed him looking at her and immediately lowered her gaze. She seemed to be frowning at her shoes before Caroline stopped in front of her. He could tell that Caroline didn't have her complete attention, and he was proven right when her brown eyes sought him out again. She quickly turned away when she noticed that he was still watching her.

That is interesting, he silently agreed with Caroline. He learned that the girl's name was Kendra, and that she was Caroline's best friend. Dominic refrained from hitting on her out of respect for Caroline, because he quickly grew fond of her. Besides, there were plenty of other girls who wanted him. Yet he found himself watching Kendra, and trying to discern if she really did have a crush on him. Her reactions to him were inconsistent. Sometimes he caught her staring at him, but she appeared to be in a bad mood rather than shy.

After almost a year of wondering, he had to know. He approached her on the first day of school and got a chilly reception. Her stony expression when they were assigned as lab partners in Chemistry class pissed him off, but he did his best to soften her attitude toward him. When that didn't work, he tried seduction. After all his best moves failed, he found a different way to raise her temperature. He could think of so many better things to do to her rather than annoy her, but he enjoyed getting a fiery reaction out of her nonetheless.

Dominic now knew that she had been fighting her hormones the entire time. She'd even had fantasies of him shutting her up during an argument by kissing her. Who knew that during lab experiments she'd actually been thinking about having sex with him? All her hot fantasies were starting to become a source of frustration for him rather than enjoyment. He wanted to do these things with her instead of just reading about them.

He needed a new sex partner, but he wanted to get Kendra out of his system first. Dominic was tired of fantasizing about her all the time. She was the only girl on his mind, and he needed to finish this thing with her. He had been obsessed with her for too long and he sure didn't want to end up like his dad, he thought bitterly.

Kendra opened her locker warily the next morning and looked immediately at the top shelf for a note from him. He watched her turn around to look for him and turn back after she saw him.

"Looking for me?" Dominic asked as he approached her.

"Never," she replied, casting a glance toward the people beside them.

"Hmm, I could have sworn that you were looking for me yesterday." He was gratified to see her blush at the memory.

"Just leave me alone, okay? I'm not in the mood today," she said.

He was disappointed that she didn't tell him off. If she wasn't attacking him physically, she was usually attacking him verbally. "What's wrong?"

She laughed without mirth. "Like you don't know."

Dominic lost patience with her. "Walk with me," he barked.

She followed him to the empty auditorium. "What happens next? Am I supposed to give you a blow job in the boys' bathroom? You didn't leave any instructions this time."

"What the hell is wrong with you?" Dominic demanded angrily.

"That's the million-dollar question, isn't it? I had a nice boyfriend, but I didn't want him. No, I had to beg the school player to fuck me. So, there is a lot wrong with me." She flopped down in a seat and carelessly spread her legs over the armrests. "Okay, let's get this over with."

He waited until he got control of his anger and moved toward her. "Take off your clothes," he commanded coldly.

She obviously hadn't expected him to take her up on her offer. "What?"

"I can't fuck you with your clothes on, can I?" He allowed his eyes to rake over her jean-clad body.

Her ridiculous refusal to back down had her looking desperately around for an excuse. "You still have your clothes on," was her weak response.

He reached down to grab hold of his t-shirt and pull it over his head. Her eyes went wide as he dropped it on the floor just as the warning bell rang. "We're going to be late," she said in a suddenly breathless voice. Her eyes slid from his abs to his face.

Dominic stepped forward. "Touch."

When she just stared at him, he repeated the word. "You wanted to touch my abs, so go ahead."

She tentatively reached out her hand and splayed it across his stomach. He forced himself to hold still as she bit her lip and ran her hand over his abs. His body reacted to her touch, and her breathing accelerated as she looked straight at the bulge in his pants. She pulled her hand back and stared up into his eyes.

He leaned down and placed his hands on her shoulders. "First of all, don't ever offer to fuck anyone unless you mean it. Second, you did not beg me to fuck you." He leaned in further to whisper in her ear. "But I'll wait until you do sweetheart."

Dominic straightened up and grabbed his t-shirt off the floor. "Oh, I'm sorry. You did say you weren't in the mood today. I'll leave you alone now."

Her breathing still wasn't back to normal as he walked away. Dominic felt like he was back on top of his game, and he smiled in triumph.

CHAPTER 10

That conceited jerk! Kendra fumed over the events of the morning for the rest of the day. Touch my abs, he had told her. The worst part was that she did. No, she corrected herself, the worst part was that thinking about the feel of his skin and the hard muscle beneath it made her want to touch him again. Her body responded to his in direct rebellion to her mind's better judgment. She hated that he had so much power over her. Yet her touch also had the power to affect him too.

What had played out between them in the auditorium had not begun as a seduction. She had been disgusted with herself and vulgar in her disdain for his lifestyle and her participation in it. He had obviously been trying to intimidate her, and she had stubbornly held on to the pretense that he hadn't succeeded.

Then everything changed when he took off his shirt to give her a mouthwatering view of his abs. She'd only gotten a brief glimpse of them in the past, but she had never forgotten it. Now he was standing right in front of her and urging her to touch him. Whatever other emotions had motivated them lifted away like steam as sultry heat flared between them. It was different than the wild passion that had swept through her like a hurricane during their past encounters. She found herself waiting in helpless anticipation for his next move. Kendra remembered her trembling excitement as a shirtless Dominic had leaned over her, and she had felt his body heat along with his warm breath as he whispered in her ear.

What he had said, though, was like the bucket of ice water that she needed to wake her up to reality. He actually expected her to beg him. Kendra resolved that it would be a cold day in hell before that ever happened. She should thank him for being such a jerk, because it had snapped her out of her glum, self-destructive mood.

Yes, she had lost her boyfriend over her infatuation with Dominic. Yes, she had made a huge mistake by giving in to her strong, irrational attraction to him. She couldn't change the past, but she could prevent further mistakes in the future. Kendra decided that the fantasies she had already fulfilled with Dominic would be her last. Since she had no interest in anyone else, she decided to forgo dating altogether for the time being and focus on other interests.

"Fencing?" Caroline looked at her like she was crazy.

"It's something I've always wanted to learn," Kendra told her.

"Since when?" Caroline asked. "You never mentioned it before."

"Well, I always thought it looked cool in movies." That had been during her Zorro phase when she was eleven, but she thought she could rekindle her interest in it by taking lessons.

Caroline looked far from convinced. "What's this about?"

"It's about fencing," Kendra said. "I want to try something new."

"I know you're upset about Homecoming, but we can still go. We want you to go with us."

Caroline's earnest expression failed to sway Kendra. "Thanks, but I really don't feel like going."

"But you already bought your dress," Caroline fretted. "Maybe Dominic—"

"Hell no!" Kendra vehemently interrupted her. "Don't you dare say anything to him about that."

"I won't mention you directly," she said. "I'll just ask him if he's going."

"No, Caroline. I mean it," Kendra warned.

"Okay, okay," she relented.

Another lunch ended with Kendra hardly eating any food. She wasn't voluptuous to begin with, not like Caroline with all her curves in all the right places. Even Veronica had more of a womanly body, although she was younger than Kendra. She wasn't rail thin, but her own curves weren't so noticeable. It made her wonder why Dominic had fixated on her instead of her friend or her sister. Of course, he had hooked up with so many different girls that she couldn't actually say that he had a type. Realizing that she was falling right back into her bad habit of thinking about him, she focused on what was going on in class.

Her relief that this school day had come to an end was marred by his presence at her locker. "You said that you were going to leave me alone."

He opened her locker for her. "I thought you might be in the mood now."

"I'm not." She placed the books she needed into her backpack.

"Fencing, huh? You know there are much better ways to work out aggression. Don't you, Kendra?"

"Yes, but those would get me arrested for assault," she replied coolly.

Dominic grinned. "You can assault me anytime you want."

"Don't tempt me," she muttered.

"I already did." Despite his words, all the cockiness was gone from his expression. "We never got to finish our discussion from this morning."

"And we never will," she declared.

"That would be a shame. You make your point so forcefully. I'm interested in hearing what else you have to say."

She wouldn't allow his darkly intense gaze to seduce her again. "I have nothing more to say to you."

He followed her out to the parking lot. "You broke up with your boyfriend for me. You wouldn't do that if you didn't want to be with me."

"My boyfriend broke up with me, because I cheated on him. You just happened to be the guy I cheated with. As for being with you, I'm not that delusional. You're not with anyone for long."

"Is that what's stopping you?" Dominic asked. "How long were you with Caleb? Did the duration make a difference when it ended? Did it make the sex any better for you?"

"That's not the point. We were a real couple," she explained. "Not just fuck buddies."

He laughed derisively. "Why? Because he took you to the movies? I can do that if you want."

"You just don't get it, do you? You have no idea what real relationships are all about," Kendra realized.

"Enlighten me," he challenged.

"It's about spending time together and getting to know each other." Caught up in her earnest explanation, she again forgot that she didn't want to speak to him.

"We spent a lot of time together last year as lab partners, and I know you very well after reading your diary. I probably know you better than anyone else," he mused.

"That's not getting to know me," she exclaimed. "That's invading my privacy."

"So, people need to know each other before they have sex, but not too well."

She scowled at him in annoyance. "Stop twisting my words around."

"I'm just trying to understand."

His attempt at looking innocent didn't fool her for a second. "No, you're not. You're trying to trick me into having sex with you."

"Like Caleb?"

Kendra glared at him. "That was different."

"How?"

She turned away from him in frustration. "I don't have to explain myself to you."

"How was it different?" Dominic demanded. "Because he put two months into wooing you? I put in a whole year."

She turned back to him with her hands on her hips. "You mean the year you spent antagonizing me? We've never dated, Dominic."

"Let's date then," he suggested.

"It doesn't work like that. Dating is not just a means to an end. It's supposed to be about—"

"Love?" Dominic interrupted with a smirk. "Tell me how in love you were with Caleb."

"I could have been in time." She didn't know why she was justifying her relationship to him. "If we could have gotten past—"

"The crappy sex?" Dominic interrupted her again.

She was so mad that she didn't bother finishing her sentence. "You asked me why I won't go out with you. This is why. That's all you ever think about."

"On the contrary," he said. "I never think about crappy sex." He stepped forward to back her up against the car. "I think about how to turn you on."

His body was too close to hers. "People are watching us." Her voice sounded somewhat panicked.

"Let's go to my house," he suggested. "We can be alone there."

"This is over, Dominic. I'm not going to be alone with you anymore." Kendra was proud of how strong her voice sounded as she looked directly into his eyes.

Dominic surprised her by smiling as he stepped back. "Hot and cold."

"What?" Kendra couldn't help asking.

"Just getting to know you," he answered. "I'll catch you on the flip side."

"The flip side of what?"

His only answer was another smile before he walked away.

"Stop talking about me to Dominic," Kendra said in exasperation to Caroline on the phone that evening.

"I didn't say anything to him about Homecoming," Caroline defended herself.

"Don't say anything about me at all to him," Kendra reiterated.

"You're my best friend. Now I can't even mention your name?" Caroline asked.

"Not to Dominic. Please just leave me out of your conversations with him," Kendra pleaded.

She didn't know if Caroline listened to her, but Dominic finally seemed to get the hint. He stopped showing up at her locker, although he still watched her if they happened to see each other in the hallways. She assumed that he had found a new girlfriend, or whatever he called the girls he hooked up with.

Caroline tried several more times to persuade her to attend Homecoming with her and Adam, but Kendra had no interest in going. She hadn't even been that excited about it when she'd had a date. Caroline seemed to be more upset about the dress that Kendra wouldn't get to wear than anything else.

"I'm sure I'll wear it to a party or something when I go to college." Kendra really didn't care if she ever wore it. She had nothing against dressing up, but she wasn't dying to either.

"This is our last year of high school. You shouldn't miss out on anything."

This had become Caroline's refrain, and Kendra was getting tired of it. "I'm having fun trying new things."

"It's great that you got into fencing, but that doesn't mean that you should miss out on senior events."

Kendra rolled her eyes. She knew that Caroline was already worried about whether Kendra would go to prom. "I'll let you go so you can start getting ready."

"There are still a few hours until the dance," Caroline said.

Kendra mock gasped. "Are you sure you'll have enough time?"

"Very funny."

Kendra laughed. "I know how you are. Anyway, have fun tonight."

"Thanks. I still wish you were going."

"I've got secret plans for tonight," Kendra joked. "So, call me tomorrow, and I'll have stories to tell."

After she hung up the phone, she decided to hang out on her computer until dinner. Her mom came upstairs about a half hour later to inform her that her date had arrived, and also to ask why she hadn't mentioned having a date tonight.

Before Kendra could say anything, her mom fired off another question. "Is that what you're wearing? I think you'd better change, because he's dressed up."

Michael couldn't possibly still want to take her to Homecoming, could he? It was too early to leave for the dance anyway. She had no answers for her mom, because she didn't know what was going on herself. "I'll go down and ask him."

She couldn't believe her eyes when she went downstairs and saw Dominic wearing a suit. All she could do was gape at him while he stood there looking like a perfect gentleman.

"Kendra, why aren't you ready?" he asked with solicitous concern.

"Ready for what?" she dared to ask. Surely, he wouldn't say something inappropriate in front of her parents. She watched in fascination as a pitiful expression appeared on his face.

"Are you standing me up? You know I made reservations at Rosewood."

Her dad whistled. "That's an expensive place."

If she didn't know better, Dominic's crestfallen expression would have fooled her too. "Are you going to make me cancel?"

Completely unaware of the predator standing before her, Kendra's mom spoke up. "Of course not. Go and get ready, Kendra."

That was how she found herself wearing her Homecoming dress and riding in Dominic's car as he spirited her away to who knew where.

CHAPTER 11

"What's with the suit?" Kendra asked as Dominic pulled out of her driveway.

"I needed to impress your parents," he answered. "How'd I do?"

He knew very well how he'd done, she stewed. "At least you're honest about it having nothing to do with me."

"How can you even say that?" Dominic wondered. "This is all about you. I'm not going out with your parents."

"You manipulated them into making me go out with you," she fumed. "They would have forbidden it if they knew what kind of guy you really are."

"Why didn't you tell them?" His eyes were on the road, but he smiled at the expression he imagined was on her face.

"Because you just showed up out of the blue with all your lies, and there would have been too much to explain," she huffed.

"I didn't lie. I do have a reservation at Rosewood," he said. "As for your parents, you didn't tell them because you didn't want them to forbid you. You wanted to go on this date with me."

Kendra couldn't believe his nerve. "I didn't even know about this so-called date until you showed up at my house."

"It was a pleasant surprise." He had to glance at her and enjoy her look of indignation. "The fact remains that you didn't have to come with me if you didn't want to. Everything that's happened between us happened because you wanted it to. Nobody made you do anything that you didn't want to do."

"You just have to keep throwing that in my face. How much I want you," she said bitterly. "Do you have any idea how obnoxious that is?"

"I'm not throwing anything in your face. I'm just trying to make you see the logic in it instead of casting me as some kind of villain."

"Oh, now you're going to use logic to convince me to sleep with you. You really are a piece of work," she exclaimed.

"What is so terrible about wanting me? It's not like it's a one-sided attraction. I want you too," he declared.

"You want every girl, and you get every girl. That's what's so terrible about it. You always get everything that you want." Kendra inwardly cringed at how childish that last sentence sounded. She might as well have proclaimed that it wasn't fair.

"I don't think logic will work on you," he noted dryly. "You just told me that you're denying yourself what you want only to keep me from getting what I want."

"That's not the only reason," she insisted.

"Okay, what other reasons do you have?" Dominic questioned. "You're not saving yourself for marriage, and you're not waiting for love."

"I made a mistake," she admitted. "I should have waited for love like Caroline did."

"What people call love is just a series of brain chemicals."

"You're such a romantic," she gushed sarcastically.

"Okay, for arguments sake, let's say love exists. What if

you're one of those people who never finds it? Does that mean that you'll never have sex again?"

"Did you kidnap me to depress me?" Kendra snapped irritably. "Since I'm not even eighteen yet, I'm a long way from never."

"When's your birthday?" Dominic asked.

"Why? Are you going to offer yourself as my present?"

How did he always goad her into saying things she would regret?

Surprisingly, he didn't jump on that with something vulgar. "I'm just making conversation and getting to know you. That's what people do on a date."

"People who are on a *real* date," she corrected him.

"I've never been on a real date before."

She had been looking out the window but whipped her head around to stare at him. "You can't be serious. You've had ten thousand girlfriends."

"I've hooked up with girls, but there certainly haven't been ten thousand of them," he answered in an amused tone.

"How the hell did you get all those girls to sleep with you without taking them out?" Kendra demanded.

"Because sex has nothing to do with movies or dinner," he explained. "It's all about attraction."

"Whatever," she grumbled. "Where are we going anyway?"

"I already told you. We're having dinner at Rosewood."

"So now you think you can buy your way into my pants," she said.

"You're the one who equates paying for dates with sex," he told her.

"That's not what I meant!"

"Calm down," he laughed. "I was just teasing you. You're also not wearing pants right now. You look lovely, by the way."

She ignored his compliment. "I bought this for Homecoming."

"Yes, Caroline told me all about your dress. It's just as pretty as she described it."

"I knew it!" Kendra fumed. "She had to whine to you about me not going to Homecoming. That's why you knew I was home today."

"Don't blame Caroline. You already told me that you broke up with Michael, and I knew you weren't going with anyone else."

"How?" Kendra asked.

"Word gets around, and I listen for any news about you," Dominic said.

"Just because I'm not going out with someone else doesn't mean that I've changed my mind about you," she stressed. "You might as well stop wasting your time."

"Since you're so sure about that, there's no harm in going out with me. Is there? Of course, I'll understand if you can't trust yourself with me."

Even though she knew he was just baiting her, she couldn't help replying indignantly, "Unlike you, I have self-control."

"Good. Then we can enjoy a pleasant evening. You're dressed like a lady, and you'll act like a lady."

"What's that supposed to mean?" Kendra bristled.

"I'm just admiring your classy dress. From what I hear, most Homecoming dresses are short. The knee length style you chose suits your innocent exterior."

She looked away from his smirk and told herself not to rise to the bait. If he was really taking her to Rosewood, she would enjoy and expensive meal and be done with him. True to his word, he had reservations at the pricey restaurant.

Kendra momentarily forgot that she was angry with him as they followed the hostess past tables draped with white linen tablecloths. Dominic even pulled out her chair for her before taking his own seat. She would never tell him for fear of inflating his ego even more, but he looked great in a suit. She could easily picture him as some big shot at a Fortune 500 company someday.

"These menus have no prices," she noticed.

"Mine does," he informed her.

"That's sexist," she complained.

"We already agreed that I'm paying," he reasoned.

"They didn't know that. They just assumed, because I'm the girl," she continued her rant.

"I thought we agreed to have a pleasant evening," he reminded her.

She held out her hand. "Let me see your menu."

"Don't worry about it. Just order what you want," he said.

"But—"

"Kendra," he interrupted her in a hushed voice. "Please don't cause a scene."

"Fine," she relented. Then she lowered her voice too. "Don't think this means I owe you anything."

He actually looked offended by her words. "You don't," he replied in an icy tone.

They fell silent as they read their menus. After the waiter took their orders, Dominic again tried to engage her in conversation. "Are you enjoying your fencing lessons?"

"Like you care," she said.

"Kendra," he hissed. "Look where we are. Polite conversation is expected here."

Feeling like a chastised child, she gave him a surly look but softened her tone. "Yes, it's a lot of fun."

"Are you learning the foil, epee, or saber?" He shrugged at her surprised expression. "I looked up a few things about it."

He studied for this date the way he studied for school, she silently mused. "The foil. It's the best for beginners, because it's the most lightweight sword."

"Are you going to enter tournaments?"

"My instructor recommends that we do, and I'm considering it," she replied. "It's really the only way to test your skills."

"The thrill of competition," he remarked.

It occurred to her that most players had a talent, like sports or music, to attract girls. Or they had that rebellious tough guy attitude that so many girls were drawn to. Dominic didn't fit into any of these categories. "Have you ever competed in anything?"

"I played baseball when I was a kid, but nothing since then. I think we're always competing against other people in life though. Right now, I'm competing with other students for college money. There are only so many scholarships to go around."

He told her that he wanted to get a business degree, and she smiled at guessing right when she had imagined him in the future. He managed to converse with her through the entire meal without once saying anything suggestive. She dropped her guard and enjoyed herself until the waiter gave him the check.

Kendra watched him pull a credit card out of his wallet. "How did you get a credit card?"

"It's my dad's," he answered.

"Does your dad pay for all your dates?" she needled him. "Oh yeah, this is your first date."

"It's my birthday, so I asked for this instead of a party."

She laughed. "Right. Today just happens to be your birthday."

He silently handed her his wallet so that she could see his driver's license.

"Happy birthday," she told him grudgingly.

"Thanks for celebrating with me," he said.

She was annoyed with herself for feeling guilty about giving him attitude on his birthday. It wasn't like she had known. "You know, you could have just asked me to go to your birthday dinner with you. I'm not that much of a—"

"I know," he cut in before she could say a swear word. "It's just more fun to mess with you. Your expression was priceless when you saw me standing in your living room."

"Jerk," she exclaimed, but her laugh was real this time.

The atmosphere between them was comfortable as they left the restaurant. When Kendra asked him where they were going when she noticed him merging onto the highway, her tone was curious rather than suspicious.

"Amish country," she repeated after he told her. "What are we going to do there at night? They don't even have electricity."

"That's exactly why we're going. It's the perfect place for stargazing. There's no light pollution to obstruct our view."

He turned on the radio to a soft rock station, and Kendra relaxed and enjoyed the ride into the dark farm country. Dominic pulled into the parking lot of a closed general store and turned off the engine. They got out of the car and stood looking at the amazing view of the night sky glittering with stars.

The chilly air prompted Dominic to take off his suit jacket and help Kendra put it on. He smiled at the image she made as his jacket engulfed her, with the sleeves dangling past her hands. He put an arm around her waist and drew her to him as they gazed up at the stars. The scene surpassed the romantic fantasies she used to have about him before she found out that he was a player.

She remembered the first time she saw him. It was her first day of high school, and she was both excited and scared about the new experience. There were so many unfamiliar faces among the throng of students. She and Caroline had giggled in nervous excitement about all the cute boys. Seeing Dominic amped up that awareness to a previously unimagined level. Kendra wouldn't have been able to laugh if she had wanted to, because her breath caught in her throat at his entrance into the room. She was seated at her desk in English class when he walked through the door. There was no clap of thunder to accompany the lightning bolt that suddenly struck her at the sight of him.

He didn't look like he belonged in the same grade as the rest of them. There was a confidence to the way he held himself that was lacking in the other boys. He exuded a cool self-assurance instead of the exaggerated swagger some of the other guys had. She watched him calmly survey the room before deciding where to sit. He showed none of the trepidation that had prompted her to choose a seat as quickly as possible.

Of course, his gorgeous dark eyes passed right over her without stopping. She knew that never in a million years could he possibly have any interest in her. A guy like that was completely out of her league. As if to prove her right, he sat down next to a pretty cheerleader type and began to say something to her. She watched them from her seat at the back of the class. The girl was definitely interested, because she smiled and flipped her hair in a flirty manner.

Kendra listened as the teacher took attendance, and she found out that his name was Dominic Miller. She thought that his masculine name suited his strong masculine presence. Despite his complete lack of awareness to her existence, she had her first fantasy about him that evening. She imagined him being the first boy to kiss her.

Kendra had written down all those romantic illusions about him in her diary. She still had that diary, and it was much different than the one Veronica had given him. It was full of sweet, innocent daydreams about a version of Dominic that didn't exist. Even after she found out the truth about him, she couldn't stop thinking about him. Her attempt at suppressing her fantasies about him had only twisted them into something more lascivious.

Now, however, those much more dangerous romantic notions were stirring in her as she stood in dreamy contemplation with his arm around her. Its sudden absence immediately drew her attention. She turned to see him fiddling with something in the car. Then she heard the music begin to play as he returned to her.

"May I have this dance?" He held out his hand to her.

She hesitated. "Here?"

"If you were at Homecoming, you'd probably be dancing under fake stars. We've got the real thing."

She took his hand and placed her other hand on his shoulder. Her heels lessened the height disparity between them. Dominic lightly gripped her waist with one hand as he gazed at her. Being in his arms felt so natural as they swayed together to the beautiful love song. She unconsciously relaxed her stiff posture and slowly drifted closer to his body. There was only the two of them beneath the canopy of stars.

Without knowing how it had happened, Kendra realized that both his hands were on the small of her back, while her arms reached up to wrap around his neck. They were dancing very close together, and nothing had ever felt so perfect. They remained in that pose after the song ended and the DJ began to talk. Kendra slowly pulled back out of his arms.

"We should head back," Dominic said.

"Yeah," she agreed after a short delay.

The romantic atmosphere didn't change during the ride back to her house while the soft music continued to play on the radio. "I'll walk you to your door," he said after pulling into her driveway.

He smiled at her as they stood on her porch. "Thank you for a lovely evening. Goodnight, Kendra."

"What's wrong?" he enquired after she just stood there looking at him instead of opening the door to her house.

She shook her head in denial. "Nothing." Her own smile was a pale imitation of his. "Thanks for dinner. Happy birthday," she told him again.

He waited until she began to walk into her house before leaving the porch. Kendra stood peeking out at him as he turned on the car and began to pull away. She couldn't believe it! Dominic hadn't tried to make a move on her all evening.

What was going on?

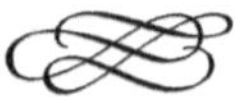

Dominic could tell that his new strategy was already having an effect on Kendra. After their discussion about dating, he had realized that it was his best option. It would take more effort than he'd ever put into seducing any girl, but he'd be damned if he'd let the inferior Caleb beat him at his own game. He already had a leg up on that loser to begin with. Kendra wanted him more than she had ever wanted Caleb. All he had to do was wait.

It was a simple plan, but it would require a lot of patience on his part. He was up to the challenge, because the reward at the end would be worth it. Dominic smiled at the irony of his situation. He had just legally become an adult, but he would have to go back to the innocence of childhood in order to seduce Kendra.

Denying himself sex was the toughest part of this plan. He couldn't take the chance of Kendra getting wind of him hooking up with another girl, so he'd have to remain celibate until this was over. That hadn't been his lifestyle since middle school. His first day of high school was also the day he lost his virginity.

Paige was a sexy brunette with fantastic legs. "Hello there.

Did you transfer from another school? I know I haven't seen you before."

Dominic hid his amazement that this older woman seemed interested in him. "I'm a freshman." He didn't like admitting that, but it would be worse to be caught in a lie. To his surprise, she didn't lose interest in him after that underwhelming news.

"You sure don't look like a freshman," she said without any subtlety about checking him out. "What's your name?"

It was true that he looked older than most of his classmates. He had been among the first guys in his grade to start developing, and he had been fortunate enough to be spared the awkward phase of adolescence on his journey to manhood. Dominic had started weight training the previous year. He didn't lift really heavy, but his consistent training had rewarded him with cut muscles that girls seemed to admire more than the huge muscles of bodybuilders.

After their sexually charged exchange in the hallway, Dominic was pumped up with confidence as he went to his next class. He spotted a cute blonde right away and took the seat beside her. She responded positively to his flirting, and he was sure that he had a shot with her. He saw her again after school and walked out of the building with her.

"Hey, Dominic. Wanna ride?" Paige's flirty expression left no doubt as to what kind of ride she was talking about.

Dominic forgot all about the cute blonde beside him as he followed Paige to her car. She drove him to her house and led him upstairs to her room. "Have you ever done this before?"

He stepped forward to kiss her. "You mean this?" He knew that he was good at kissing.

Dominic had a moment of complete amazement after they were both naked. He had previously only gotten to second base with girls, and here was this girl opening her beautiful legs and letting him into the forbidden zone. He found pure bliss there.

"Now that you got that out of your system, let's see what you can do for me."

"That wasn't good for you?" He hated to fail at anything. "Tell me what I did wrong."

"It was a good start," she said diplomatically. "You'll be able to last longer this time."

She climaxed during their second go, and Dominic loved the sense of accomplishment that gave him. He went home to research ways to please a woman.

Paige was talking to some guy in the hallway the next morning when Dominic boldly pulled her aside to whisper into her ear what he wanted to do to her.

"I'll hold you to that promise," she said with a sexy smile.

He became notorious overnight for hooking up with a senior. It only lasted two weeks, but he came away from the experience a consummate lover for a guy his age. Paige wasn't shy about telling him what she wanted. Her instruction, combined with his enthusiasm and imagination, made it easy for him to seduce other girls. Kendra was the only one who had ever given him any real trouble in that department. He was now determined to do whatever it took to have her.

Dominic soon realized that he needed a job. He couldn't expect his dad to keep paying for his dates with Kendra. His options weren't very appealing, but he couldn't expect to land a great job until after college. He found work as a stock boy in one of those wholesale warehouse stores. At least lifting all those boxes helped to keep him in shape. His fit body was a major turn on for Kendra, he knew.

Yet she mentioned his eyes in her diary more frequently than anything else. She described their nearly hypnotic power over her and called them midnight eyes. Kendra wrote that she loved the way he looked at her. It gave him a rush to read her words and know that just a glance could excite her.

He waited a couple of weeks until he approached Kendra

again. Part of his strategy involved keeping her guessing. "Would you like to come over Friday night and watch a movie with me? I'm sorry that I can't take you out to the movies yet. I'm still waiting on my first paycheck."

"Where do you work?" Kendra asked. She barely took a breath before firing off her next question. "Will your dad be home?"

"No, he has a date." Dominic had made sure of his dad's plans before he asked Kendra. "What's wrong? Afraid you'll jump me?" He smirked in the way he knew annoyed her.

"Keep dreaming. I'll come over if you promise not to try anything."

Her expression left no doubt as to her suspicion of his intentions. He was looking forward to proving her wrong.

Dominic was dressed casually in jeans and a t-shirt when he picked her up this time. Kendra also wore jeans, but she had paired them with a soft sweater that he longed to touch. Spending so much time with her and not touching her was going to be torture for him, but he was convinced that this plan would work. Doing the opposite of what she expected him to do would confuse her. She would begin to question her opinion of him.

Focusing on the movie proved to be very difficult with Kendra sitting right beside him on the couch. He could control his actions, but he couldn't control his thoughts about her. She kept sneaking glances at his lap.

"I can't control my body's reaction to you," he finally told her. "I'm sorry if that makes you uncomfortable."

"Oh, I didn't even notice," she lied in a slightly breathy voice.

"It'll be easier to hang out in public places," he continued. "We can go out on another real date after I get paid."

"Why are you doing this?" Kendra asked curiously.

He smiled in the way he knew didn't annoy her. "I want to spend more time with you." Dominic prided himself on being able to pull off this whole thing without telling her any lies. He certainly wasn't going to use Caleb's I-think-I'm-falling-for-you line.

"This movie sucks. Give me a tour of your house," she suggested impulsively.

He played along with a silly tour guide routine. "And here is the master bathroom," he announced with a flourish as he showed her their one and only bathroom.

"At least you don't have to share it with Veronica," she commented with a mock shudder. "I swear she has every hair product known to man. She is single-handedly responsible for the depletion of the ozone layer."

Dominic laughed. "She does seem high maintenance. Are you sure you guys are related?"

"Hey," she protested as she self-consciously smoothed her hair. "What are you trying to say?"

"I'm saying I prefer your natural beauty. I like to run my fingers through hair that doesn't have a bunch of glop in it."

He cleared his throat. It wasn't his intention to go down that road, so he changed the subject. "Would you like to see my room?" Damn, he hadn't meant to say it in that tone. He quickly adopted his tour guide voice to put her at ease. "Here you will find stunning views of our neighbor's garage."

It pleased him to make her laugh. He liked seeing her drop her guard and enjoy herself.

"You do have stunning views," she said as she gazed at the pictures on his wall. "I have to admit I'm surprised. I thought your room would be plastered with posters of girls in bikinis."

"These are some of the places I want to visit." He stood beside her and gazed at the picture of a white sand beach against the backdrop of blue-green ocean. "This is Fiji."

She moved to the next picture of a snow-covered mountain range.

"Those are the French Alps," he informed her.

Kendra studied all the pictures as he named the locations. "You like to travel, huh?"

"I will," he said. "I haven't been anywhere yet."

"You never went on any family vacations?" she asked.

"My dad's pretty practical. He decided he'd rather save up money for college and to buy me a car. I would actually rather have the car than a few postcards and pictures. He did take me camping and fishing around here though," he explained.

"I guess I'm lucky, because I got the vacations and the car. Although the car is used," she quickly added. "We didn't go to a lot of places, but my parents did take us to Disney World and Niagara Falls."

Her eyes scanned the pictures on his bedroom wall again before she looked at him and smiled. "I think you'll get to go to these places."

He noticed the merry twinkle in her eyes. "You do, huh? What makes you think so?"

"Because you get everything that you want," she teased and flitted out of the room.

She had entered his dad's room before he could stop her. Sobering quickly, he walked over to stand beside her and face the photograph that had caught her attention. He usually avoided looking at it. There were more in the photo album downstairs, but he never looked at those anymore.

"You look just like her," Kendra said in wonder. "She's beautiful."

"Time to go." He didn't quite succeed in keeping the hard edge out of his voice.

She placed a hand on his arm. "I'm sorry. I didn't mean to intrude."

"It's not your fault," he said in a gentler tone. "I don't really come in here much."

He turned away from the dresser. "You know, it just doesn't

have the elegant ambiance of my room." The tour guide act fell flat, because he wasn't feeling it anymore.

Once again, he made no move to kiss her after he drove her home, but this time it had more to do with his mood than his seduction strategy.

That was their last date at his house, but they began to see each other often. They went out to the movies and to dinner, although at much more affordable places than Rosewood.

"I need to get a job too," Kendra decided. "It's not fair for you to pay all the time."

"You can cook for me sometimes. After all, a woman's place is in the kitchen," he joked to arouse her ire.

He really made fun of her when she got hired as a waitress at a burger joint. "Well, if you can't cook it, at least you can serve it."

"Shut up, Neanderthal."

"Is that any way to treat a paying customer? Bring me my milkshake, woman." He laughed at the dirty look she gave him.

"Be careful, or I'll dump it over your head," she threatened.

He thought that it would seem like forever as he waited, but the time went much faster than he had expected. They joked, argued, and had serious discussions about life.

"How many kids do you want?" Kendra asked him during a study date at her house one day.

"I don't want any kids," he replied. "How many do you want?"

"Two. How could you not want any kids? What about your wife? I'm sure she'll want kids," she insisted.

"No, she won't, because I'm not getting married."

She looked even more flabbergasted by that statement. "Why not? Don't you want to share your life with someone?"

"I'm sure I'll meet lots of interesting people," he said. "I don't have to tie myself down to just one."

Kendra rolled her eyes. "Oh, of course. You can't be satisfied with one woman."

"Society places an unrealistic expectation of monogamy on us. Most relationships don't have that kind of staying power. Hence the fifty percent divorce rate in this country."

"That also means that fifty percent stay together," she countered. "You can choose to be an optimist or a pessimist about it."

"I'm neither," he told her. "I'm a realist. Passion can't last a lifetime. They even have a term for its duration—the honeymoon phase."

She nodded. "That's why you have to have more than passion to sustain the relationship. You need love and friendship."

"I'd rather have passion and excitement."

"Okay," she said with a laugh. "Moving on."

They were moving on, but he wasn't sure to what. She had unblocked his number, and she even took the initiative to call him and wish him a merry Christmas. He called her at midnight on New Year's Eve, and she eagerly answered his call. They had become so close that Dominic was the only other friend she invited to her birthday dinner along with Caroline and her boyfriend.

"It's your eighteenth birthday. How could you not want a party?" Caroline complained again.

"Dominic didn't have a party either," Kendra said.

"You two are a perfect pair," Caroline grumbled.

"Cheer up," Dominic urged. "We can embarrass her at the restaurant by singing Happy Birthday really loud."

"Don't even think about it," Kendra warned.

Winter was giving way to spring when it dawned on Dominic that he hadn't had sex for six months. He wasn't even sure what he was doing anymore. Maybe he had miscalculated this whole thing with Kendra. Perhaps ceasing all flirting with her wasn't the way to go. How could he expect to seduce her if there was absolutely nothing sexual at all between them?

He still felt an attraction to her, but she had probably stopped thinking of him that way. Instead of romancing her, he had ended up in the friendship zone. He would have to rethink his strategy.

"Can I come over your house after school today? Veronica wants the house to herself." Kendra gave him a meaningful look, and he understood that her sister was kicking her out of the house so she could have sex with her boyfriend.

"Sure," he agreed.

"Will I get to meet your dad this time?"

"Sorry," he apologized. "My dad went to Vegas. He'll be back on Sunday, so you can come over for dinner then and meet him."

"Oh, okay."

She seemed lost in thought, and he wondered if she felt slighted by him for not introducing her to his dad sooner. That was something that he should have considered, but it hadn't occurred to him that she would want to meet him.

Having her come to his house should have been Dominic's suggestion in the first place. He might have gotten somewhere with her by now if they were alone more often. His aggression hadn't worked on her, but there was such a thing as being too passive.

Kendra arrived, and he offered her something to drink. She accepted the soda and took a sip. "So, I was wondering something?"

"Yes?" Dominic prompted after she failed to continue.

"How come you stopped trying to have sex with me?" The words came out of her in a rush. She looked down at her feet before tilting her head to look at him under her lashes.

His heart started to beat faster, and he became extremely

aware of their proximity on the couch. "You said that you didn't want to. Have you changed your mind?"

"No," she answered quickly. "But kissing would be okay."

"Yeah?" He took her soda and set it on the coffee table.

Dominic cautioned himself to go slow. If he pushed her too far now, he might not get another chance. He was just going to brush his lips against hers to start, but his long-denied passion was too strong. Her parted lips were too inviting, and his tongue plunged into her mouth. He was easing her down onto the seat cushions within seconds. His hand slipped under her shirt to find her breast. She moaned, inflaming him further.

"Stop," she gasped when his mouth moved to replace his hand on her cleavage.

Cursing himself for losing control, he sat back on the far end of the couch and allowed her to sit up. He waited for Kendra to yell at him. His plan had finally started to work, but he had ruined it by moving too fast.

"That didn't turn out the way I planned," she said with a laugh.

He looked at her in surprise. "You're not mad at me?"

"No," she stated. "You were right that everything happened because I wanted it. You were the one who was okay with being just friends."

"So, we're okay?" Dominic asked.

"Yeah," she agreed. "But I better leave." She glanced down at the bulge in his pants.

"I'll be okay in a few minutes," he told her. "Then we can go somewhere else. I know, we'll go to your place of employment, and you can make me a milkshake."

"Sorry, but I'm off the clock. You'll have to find yourself another waitress."

Dominic thought about Kendra that night. She was still attracted to him, but he wasn't sure what to do about it. Even though she had admitted that she wanted it, nothing had really changed. She was still stopping herself from having sex with him. Maybe it was time to admit defeat. He was tired of denying himself sex, and he obviously wasn't going to get it from her.

He was getting ready for school the next morning when someone rang the doorbell. Dominic opened the door to find Kendra on his doorstep.

"Hey! So, I thought we could have a senior cut day."

He grinned. "You're on. What do you want to do?"

"Oh," she said in a shaky voice that ruined her attempt at casual sexiness. "I can think of a few things."

He momentarily lost all his game as he stood rooted to the spot in fear of doing or saying the wrong thing.

"Well," she prompted. "Aren't you going to invite me in?"

CHAPTER 13

Kendra was sure that she had been less nervous during her first time. She had used up all of her courage walking into Dominic's house, and she now sagged against the front door with her eyes closed. The look of panic she had seen in his eyes hadn't helped to inspire her own confidence.

"Look at me, Kendra," his familiar voice coaxed sensually.

She opened her eyes to meet his dark, smoldering gaze. Excitement heightened her senses, and her nervousness turned into thrilling anticipation. Everything intensified, from her heartbeat to her breathing, as Dominic closed the short distance between them.

His hungry kiss engulfed her in flames of desire. The fire consumed them both while their hands desperately sought contact with feverish skin. Clothes were a hindrance that they impatiently yanked out of their way.

"You're so wet," Dominic hissed in her ear while his finger slipped inside her.

Kendra fumbled inside her purse, which was still miraculously hanging from her shoulder, and found the box of condoms she had stopped to buy before driving to his house. She wordlessly handed it to Dominic and pulled the purse off her shoulder to drop it on the floor. He ripped open the box and pulled out a foil packet. Her eyes followed his movements as he tore it open and put on the condom.

Then he lifted her up in a mirror image of what he had done to her in the school bathroom as he leaned her against the door and tilted her hips to accommodate him. There were no barriers this time to stop his erection from unerringly reaching its goal. Kendra moaned as he filled her and began to thrust within her.

"So fucking hot," he groaned.

He had slowed his pace to find a rhythm that would please her. His kisses were now deep and slow as an unbearable need for release built within her. Kendra's moans became more desperate as she clung to him.

"Come for me sweetheart," he urged huskily.

She cried out as she reached her peak and clenched around him. Dominic moaned and began to thrust furiously before stiffening and coming with a groan. They stayed in that position while they took in short, gasping breaths.

He then kissed her lightly on the lips before disengaging their bodies. Kendra's panties slid down to her ankles as Dominic set her down. She had worn a skirt that he had merely lifted out of his way before yanking down her panties. He hadn't bothered removing his own clothes either. His jeans were hanging down his legs along with his underwear.

He went to dispose of the condom, while she took a moment to set her clothes right. Then she turned toward the door and reached for the doorknob.

"Where are you going?" Dominic asked sharply.

She turned to look at him. "I thought that..."

"That what?" he demanded.

"Well, you got what you wanted, so..." Kendra trailed off helplessly again.

"What I wanted." He scowled at her. "Oh, that's right. I'm the bad guy. Hell, I'm even going to kick you out right after fucking you."

"I didn't say that," she protested. "It's just that…"

He stalked toward her. "It's what, Kendra?"

"I thought, I mean, I thought," she stammered under his intimidating gaze. "That you're done with me," she finished in a small voice.

His jaw clenched, and his dark eyes burned with such intensity that Kendra involuntarily took a step back. He moved with the lazy grace of a panther as he trapped her against the door. "No, Kendra," he growled, "I'm not done with you."

His searing kiss belied the fact that they had just spent their passion only moments ago. He took her hand to lead her silently up to his bedroom. This time they undressed completely, and she got to touch him everywhere that she had wanted to for so long. Their pace now was unhurried as they savored the feel of skin on skin while they explored each other's bodies.

Feeling sated and satisfied as she lay on the bed beside Dominic, Kendra smiled at him. "I'm hungry," she announced.

"So am I," he teased, nibbling on her earlobe.

"Okay," she said, "you've proven you're insatiable. But I need some food. I was too nervous to eat breakfast."

"Alright, I'll take you out for breakfast." He slid his hand between her thighs. "I'll have dessert later."

He grinned wickedly at still having the power to make her blush after what they had just done.

Kendra opted for French toast, because she didn't want to eat anything too heavy. The way Dominic was looking at her brought back her nervous tension. She had expected him to become indifferent to her after she gave into him, but it seemed she had instead unleashed the sexy beast within him.

"Aren't you going to have anything?" she asked after he only ordered coffee.

"Yes," he answered as he held her captive with his dark gaze. "I will."

She couldn't understand how he could unnerve her so much after she'd already had sex with him twice. He had been so friendly and easygoing for all these months that she had almost forgotten about his sexually aggressive side. By the time they arrived back at his house, the atmosphere between them was charged with sexual tension.

"Do you mind if I take a shower?" Kendra asked.

"Take your time," he offered. "We have all day."

She gulped. How many times could he possibly have sex in one day? Scurrying away into the bathroom, she wished that she had brought a change of underwear. She supposed that she could just leave them off until she went home. It wasn't like she needed to be modest around Dominic anymore.

Kendra lingered in the hot shower as she nervously wondered what else he expected her to do. She hoped that he wasn't going to pressure her into trying anything kinky. Her experience was limited to basic intercourse, but she imagined that he'd had all kinds of wild sex.

She was finally forced to leave the shower when the water turned lukewarm. Kendra pulled open the shower curtain and stepped out of the tub. She was startled to see how steamy the bathroom was, because she distinctly remembered turning on the fan before taking her shower. It wasn't running now, however, and she wondered if it broke while she was standing under the spray of water. Just as she was reaching for a towel, Dominic opened the door and walked into the bathroom.

Kendra felt incredibly exposed, even though he had already seen her naked. She fought the urge to cover herself as his eyes raked over her body.

"This seems familiar," he said in a low, husky voice. "Almost like we've done it before."

Her body temperature rose as she got what he was referring to. She remembered her fantasy about him walking in on her after her shower. "Did you turn off the fan?" she asked in an uneven voice.

"Steamy bathroom." He moved toward her. "Dripping wet body."

Her heart thundered as his eyes held her immobile.

"Too weak to move." He knelt down on the floor in front of her and swirled his tongue around her nipple. Then he began to suck on it.

She thought her knees might buckle, but he stood up and swept her into his arms. "I can't wait to taste you," he rasped as he carried her to his bedroom.

He deposited her on the bed and knelt down in front of it. She sat up and started scooting back in alarm. "You don't need to—"

"I want to. I've been fantasizing about this for a long time."

Dominic got up and moved to sit beside her on the bed. He placed his arm around her waist. "Please let me. I promise you'll like it." He spoke into her neck as he nuzzled her.

She didn't reply, and he tilted her head toward him and kissed her. His hand came up to caress her breast as he slowly leaned her back into the mattress. He was soon back to sucking on her nipples, and she lost herself in the sensations. His mouth trailed from her breasts down to her stomach.

When had he maneuvered himself between her legs? Just as she was about to stop him, she felt his wet, velvety tongue on her clit. Kendra gasped and tried to move away, but he held her firmly while his tongue continued to lick her most sensitive spot. She began to moan in pleasure at this incredible new feeling. Her whole body shuddered with the force of her climax.

"I knew you'd taste good." Dominic climbed back up on the

bed. His hands caressed her thighs as he watched the expression on her face. "You seemed to like that."

She wondered if she was now obligated to reciprocate. "Do you, um—"

"Relax sweetheart," he soothed. "Just enjoy the ride." He thrust into her and quickly flipped her over so that she was astride him.

Kendra had never been on top like this before, and she was unsure of herself. She sat motionless as she stared down at him.

"Do what feels good," he told her. "You'll find your rhythm."

It was awkward for her at first, and she felt self-conscious about bouncing around on top of him. His lust-filled gaze soon began to turn her on again. She had always liked the sexy way he looked at her. After a while, however, she pretty much forgot that he was there as she gave herself over to her steadily building orgasm.

Once she came down from her high, she realized that she didn't know if she should keep going. "Did you, uh, did you come?"

"Fuck yeah, I came," he exclaimed. "Hot damn, Kendra. That was the hottest fucking thing I've ever seen!"

She thought that he was the hottest thing she'd ever seen, but she didn't voice her thoughts out loud. Dominic went to dispose of the condom and take a quick shower, and Kendra got dressed. She decided to put on her panties anyway, because she just wasn't comfortable walking around without them.

They spent the next few hours relaxing in front of the TV and eating pizza. Dominic walked her out to her car and kissed her. "That was a highly productive day. We should do this again."

"We can't cut every day. Besides, your dad's coming back soon," she reminded him.

"I might have to lock him out of the house. Unfortunately, I need him to feed me. With your lack of culinary skills, we'd be living on fast food all the time."

"I can cook," she informed him indignantly. "I just don't feel obligated to cook for you. Anyway, this is your house. You should be the one to cook for me, you sexist jerk."

"You are so fun to rile up," he laughed. "Let me tell you a secret sweetheart." He leaned in to whisper in her ear. "I've got a few more skills to show you."

She again became aware of her need to change her underwear. "I think I've seen all the skills I can handle in one day."

"I was talking about cooking." He smirked.

"Sure you were."

"Kendra, it's not my fault that you have a dirty mind."

"Oh, it's completely your fault," she said as she pulled him into another kiss.

As promised, she got to meet his dad on Sunday.

"I was almost a millionaire," Mr. Miller said.

"Everyone in Vegas is almost a millionaire," Dominic commented. "At least until they lose all their money."

"Did you lose all your money?" Kendra asked in concern.

"Only my spending money," Mr. Miller assured her. "Never bet more than you can afford to lose."

"I'd rather not play if I'm going to lose," Dominic stated.

"Wow, this is the best lasagna I've ever tasted," Kendra complimented Mr. Miller.

"Dominic made it."

"Told you," Dominic gloated.

"You told her what?" his dad asked.

"Kendra didn't believe that I can cook."

"I was wrong," she admitted.

Dominic shrugged. "I found a good recipe. You can learn pretty much anything with some research."

Kendra was sure that Dominic would tire of her and take up with another girl, but it didn't happen. They continued to be lovers, and he even asked her to prom. This prompted Caroline to declare that he was in love with her. Kendra gave her a withering look.

"I just knew that you were the right woman for him," Caroline gushed.

"Please tell me that you haven't said anything like that to him," Kendra demanded anxiously.

"Geez, Kendra, give me a little credit," Caroline huffed. "He'll realize it on his own. You'll see."

Kendra didn't allow herself to entertain any such thoughts. She lived entirely in the moment when it came to Dominic. The present was all they had, and she enjoyed every moment they were together. She wasn't going to make a big deal out of going to prom with him. Being at the dance with him was lovely, but it wasn't as special as their first date.

"It was better dancing under the stars," he said as if reading her mind.

"It's always better when it's just the two of us," she agreed.

He pulled her close as they swayed together. "I say we skip the after party."

Her desire for him hadn't lessened one bit. "You might be able to persuade me."

"Persuading you is half the fun," he spoke seductively.

"What's the other half?"

"After I persuade you." He kissed her right there in the midst of their classmates, and she let him.

They continued seeing each other after graduation. Dominic had been awarded his scholarship, and Kendra had been accepted to the college where she had applied. Caroline and Adam were going to attend college together.

Kendra tried not to think about this being their last real summer together. She didn't want them all to grow apart with distance. Caroline insisted that they would keep in touch just as much as they did now. All three of them attended Kendra's first fencing tournament. She lost, but she had lots of fun.

"That's kind of sexy," Dominic told her when he saw her in her fencing gear. "You should wear that later."

"Pervert," she laughed.

"That's why you like me."

Kendra had never stopped to consider why she liked him so much. He was certainly not the only good-looking guy she had ever met, nor was he the only intelligent guy she knew. She doubted that she would ever be able to pinpoint the exact reason. Maybe it came down to chemistry, just like Dominic had said it did.

Their college departure dates were fast approaching when he told her goodbye. He had driven her home after another date. He reached over and pulled an envelope out of the glove box. "This is for you. Open it later," he said to stop her from tearing it open.

"Kendra, my dad and I are going camping before I leave for college."

"Oh," she said. "Yeah, that'll be nice for you to spend some family time together before you go."

"I probably won't see you again before I leave."

Here it was, the moment she had expected since this whole thing began. "Yeah, I'm gonna be busy too."

"I hope you have a great college experience."

His smile looked heartbreaking to her right now. She wished he'd smirk in that annoyingly obnoxious way. It would make this easier. "You too."

"Goodbye, Kendra. Take care of yourself sweetheart."

It almost undid her—him calling her sweetheart. Yet she found the strength to say farewell with dignity. "Goodbye, Dominic. Have fun in Fiji."

It was all she could manage before she gave him a fleeting smile and exited his car with the envelope clutched in her hand.

She didn't turn around to see him drive away, but went straight into the house and up to her room. Then she sat down on her bed and opened the envelope.

Kendra,

I never break my promises, because I rarely make any. I'm sorry that the first promise I'm breaking is the one I made to you, but I'll keep your diary over the yearbook I know I'll never look at again. When I think of high school, I'll always think of you.

Dominic

She wasn't going to cry, damn it! She had known all along that it would end. Vowing that these would be the first and last tears she would ever shed over him, Kendra gave in to her sadness.

She would eventually throw away the diary excerpts with his explicit notes, because she knew it wasn't right to keep something like that from another man when she had a boyfriend. The prom pictures were at home in a photo album at her parents' house. She was never able to part with Dominic's goodbye note, however. Kendra kept that tucked away in her diary of foolishly romantic girlish illusions.

CHAPTER 14

"*Y*ou need to get laid girlfriend."

This charming proclamation was made by Kendra's roommate, Samantha. She seemed to live for partying, which meant that she was constantly going out. Kendra was rarely home herself, but it was for an entirely different reason.

"I'm too tired to even think about sex," she replied as she relaxed on the couch with a bowl of ice cream.

"This is ridiculous," Samantha exclaimed. "All you do is work. You're only twenty-five, but you never have any fun. How can you stand it?"

"It'll be worth it in the end," Kendra said. That was something she told herself every day, but she wasn't sure if she believed it anymore.

She had loaded her schedule with classes and gone to school all year, so that she could finish college in three years. Then she had dived into the demanding study load of law school. After she passed the bar exam and became a lawyer, Kendra thought that she could finally relax. Her hefty student loan, however, made her postpone her dream of becoming a prosecutor to accept a job at a lucrative law firm.

It was bad enough that her boyfriend had gotten her the job, because his uncle was a senior partner there. After all her talk of female independence, she had relied on a romantic connection in her desperation to start paying off her debt. A few months later, Craig had blindsided her with a marriage proposal. He was still in medical school, so she had assumed they'd wait until he graduated before they got married. She had shocked him and herself by refusing his proposal.

"Don't you love me?"

The hurt in his eyes broke her heart. "I do, but I'm not ready to get married."

Craig didn't believe her. He said that she would want to marry him if she truly loved him. They broke up, and Kendra waited to get fired. She was prepared for it when Mr. Douglas called her into his office a couple of weeks later.

Being a no-nonsense kind of guy, he came straight to the point. "I was sorry to hear about you and my nephew. You made a fine couple."

"Yes sir," Kendra answered, dreading what was to come.

"Well, that's your personal business. As long as it doesn't affect your work performance, it's no concern of mine."

She looked at him in surprise. "Oh, it won't. Thank you, sir."

"You have a strong work ethic, Kendra. That's a very valuable asset in an employee. I may have hired you on my nephew's recommendation, but I wouldn't have kept you on if you hadn't proven yourself. This is a business, first and foremost."

"Thank you, sir. I won't let you down," she promised.

Kendra felt an even bigger obligation to do a good job after that, and she had given up her already meager social life to put in as many hours as possible at the firm. The work was tedious and far different from the thrill she would have gotten from winning criminal cases. The only reward in corporate law was financial. She told herself that it was only temporary until she paid off her student loan. Then she would pursue her dreams.

"You can't keep going at this pace," Samantha told her. "You're gonna have a nervous breakdown if you don't let loose a little."

"So, sex prevents nervous breakdowns?" Kendra asked in amusement.

"It's the best stress reliever known to man," Samantha said.

"I knew someone like you once," Kendra commented dryly.

"Who?" Samantha asked.

Kendra shook her head. "Never mind."

For a fleeting moment, she wondered what Dominic was doing now. Had he been to Fiji yet? She quickly shut down those thoughts. Everything was depressing enough as it was without a bittersweet walk down memory lane.

She was completely down on relationships right now. Even the one she had thought would last forever had ended in heartbreak. Kendra had expected to be a bridesmaid at Caroline and Adam's wedding, but that would never happen. Adam had broken up with her during their second year of college. He told her that he wanted to see other people.

"I thought that we were perfect together," Caroline had cried over the phone. "We were each other's one and only, but I guess that's why he wants to be with someone else now."

Kendra decided that sex was the root of all evil. Your sexual appetite was what led you astray and down the path to heartbreak. "He'll realize he made a mistake," she soothed.

"Well, I can be with someone else too," Caroline declared defiantly. "There's a party tonight, and I'm going. Fuck this crying over him crap!"

"Please don't do anything you'll regret," Kendra pleaded.

She could count on one hand the number of times she had heard Caroline swear, so she knew how intense her emotions had to be right now. "Listen, just hold tight. I'm gonna get on the next plane over there."

"Don't be silly. You can't afford that. Besides, I'll be fine. I'm gonna go have some fun and forget about this whole thing."

Caroline wouldn't listen to reason, and Kendra cursed the distance between them. She was on the east coast, and Caroline was going to college in Phoenix. By the time Kendra found the next available flight and made it out there, it was too late.

Since she wasn't used to drinking, it hadn't taken much for Caroline to get drunk. She then hooked up with a hot guy she had met at the party. Kendra found her crying her eyes out in her dorm the next day.

"Do you remember what happened?" she asked anxiously.

"I wish I could forget," Caroline wailed.

"Did he force himself on—"

"No! I was all over him, Kendra. God, I'm such a slut," she cried. "A total stranger, and I…"

She covered her face with her hands in shame.

Kendra put her arm around Caroline and tried to comfort her. "It was the alcohol. You weren't yourself."

"That's just an excuse," Caroline exclaimed.

She dropped her hands but wouldn't look directly at Kendra. "I've been lusting after him for a while."

Kendra regarded her in confusion. "I thought you said he was a stranger."

"He's in my Human Behavior class, but I've never talked to him before last night."

"So, it wasn't a random hookup," Kendra commented.

Caroline took a shuddering breath. "He's got these amazing blue eyes. I feel like I get lost in them when he looks at me."

"I know what that's like." Kendra had a distant expression on her face as she pictured a specific pair of midnight eyes.

The point is that I was lusting after him while I was still with Adam," Caroline admitted. "I'm a total slut."

"You're not," Kendra insisted.

She then confessed everything to Caroline about lusting after Dominic even after she had sex with Caleb. Kendra's shame was even greater when she revealed that she'd had sex with Dominic.

"Oh, I knew that," Caroline said. "The heat between you made it obvious. I didn't know that you slept with Caleb though. Why didn't you tell me?"

"I was ashamed," Kendra told her. "We agreed to wait until we were in love."

"Don't feel bad," Caroline consoled her. "I just broke that rule too. I feel like I cheated on Adam, because I had the hots for Jason before we broke up."

"Dominic said that monogamy couldn't last," Kendra remembered.

"That's a depressing thought," Caroline said.

"My parents did it," Kendra noted.

"So did mine." Caroline sighed. "I thought I would have what they have."

"This doesn't mean that you won't," Kendra reassured her. "You'll fall in love again."

She felt like a fraud saying that, since she had never been in love herself.

Caroline couldn't think beyond the present. "How am I ever going to face Jason again after the way I acted last night?"

"Hey, you weren't having sex by yourself. He was a willing participant. Guys never feel ashamed about having sex. Why should we?"

"At least he had enough sense to use a condom. I don't know what I would have done if I had to worry about that too." Caroline shuddered at the unwanted possibilities.

"You can skip class with me. C'mon, let's go stuff our faces," Kendra urged.

Caroline gave her a watery smile. "You're such a great friend to drop everything and fly here for me."

"Don't cry about that now too. I've been burned out and craving a break anyway."

That had been five years ago, and it was the last time she'd blown off her responsibilities to hang out with a friend. Caroline had recovered from her heartbreak, and her fling with Jason. That one-night stand had turned into a two-month affair before the passion between them fizzled. She had remained single for a year after that until she started dating another guy she met at college. That relationship ended when he got a job offer in another state after graduation. Caroline was currently dating a coworker, and she seemed happy again.

Kendra had also been asked out by a coworker but had turned him down, because she didn't want to complicate her work situation further. Besides, she had neither the time nor the inclination to begin a new relationship right now.

She did need to do something for stress relief, as Samantha had suggested. At least in college, she still had fencing to help her let off steam and keep in shape. Of course, she'd also had a boyfriend at the time. Kendra now wondered how she'd managed to make time for everything. Since starting work at the law firm, she'd let everything else fall by the wayside. She would have to look into joining a gym. The only exercise she got was her walk to catch the bus to work. With all her other expenses, she couldn't afford a car.

Unable to convince her to go out prowling for hot guys, Samantha left without her. She said that she was meeting some friends at a bar. Kendra looked forward to being able to sleep in. Sunday was her day to relax and recharge for the coming work-week. Her sleep was interrupted by wild sex at three o'clock in the morning.

"Shh," Samantha said but giggled loudly in the next room. "My roommate's asleep."

"Maybe she'll join us," a male voice said.

"Pervert," Samantha laughed.

"Don't worry baby, I can please you both."

"You just worry about pleasing me," Samantha demanded.

Kendra covered her ears and tried to go back to sleep. She was finally forced to take a sleeping pill in order to doze off. Fortunately, the guy was gone when she carefully ventured out of her room at noon the next day.

Samantha was painting her nails in their tiny living room. "Hey, looks like you got a good night's sleep."

Like the previous times she had been awakened by Samantha's escapades, Kendra didn't mention anything about what she had heard. "Yeah, I was out like a light."

"No wonder. They work you like a slave at that place. You should ask for a raise."

Kendra smiled ruefully at that suggestion. "I'm making the works for breakfast. Pancakes, bacon, and eggs. Want some?"

"I wish I could, but not all of us are lucky enough to have your fast metabolism," Samantha declared with envy.

Kendra thought better of admitting that she skipped lunch most of the time and felt too lazy to eat dinner sometimes by the time she got home in the evening. Samantha would just get on her case again about working too much. Even though she just wanted to have a lazy Sunday afternoon at the apartment, she gave in to Samantha's insistence that they needed to go shopping.

"Spring is here! You need some new outfits to get in the mood."

Kendra balked at the prices in the stores Samantha dragged her to. "I can't afford this."

"That's what credit cards are for," Samantha replied breezily.

"I'm in enough debt already." Kendra returned the dress she had been eyeing to the rack with all the other lovely clothes she couldn't buy.

"Fine," Samantha relented grudgingly, "we'll go check out some of the discount shops."

Kendra found two dresses and several skirts and tops for work. She smiled, admitting to herself that the shopping trip had succeeded in lifting her spirits.

"Those are sexy," Samantha commented sarcastically.

"You know I have to dress conservatively at work," Kendra reminded her.

Samantha threw up her hands in agitation. "I give up."

Kendra wore one of her new outfits to work on Monday. It was a navy-blue skirt with a matching blazer. She had paired it with a white blouse. It did make her feel nice to wear something new, even if Samantha didn't approve of the style. She soon forgot about everything else as she became bogged down in the details of her job.

"Kendra!" The receptionist interrupted her hours later in an excited whisper.

Trying to hide her annoyance, Kendra looked up at her. Kelly reminded her a lot of Samantha. As one of the few women in the office, and the youngest one at that, Kendra seemed to be the chosen one for Kelly to share gossip with. "What?"

"Oh my God," Kelly continued in the same excited whisper. "One of the hottest guys I've ever seen just went into Emery's office."

"That's great." Kendra turned her attention back to her work, hoping to end this high school conversation. She was trying to present a professional image, and Kelly wasn't helping.

"Kendra." Kelly actually grabbed her arm in her excitement. "He was checking you out."

She had to put a stop to this immediately. "Even if he was, I'm not interested. I don't date clients."

"You have to see him," Kelly continued. "I'll ring your phone when he comes out, and you can check him out while you pretend to talk."

This was becoming ridiculous. "No," she said firmly. "I'm not paid to ogle guys. Please let me do my job."

Kelly's face fell in disappointment. "Okay, but you're missing out. I can't even explain to you how hot he is."

Kendra exhaled in relief as Kelly went back to her desk. She was engrossed in her work when somebody interrupted her again sometime later.

"Hello, Kendra. I thought that was you."

Her heart seemed to stop in that instant when she heard his voice. Then she looked up into the familiar midnight eyes. "Dominic," she said in a breathy voice that didn't sound professional at all.

CHAPTER 15

She had imagined this moment. Of course she had. It had never played out this way in her imagination though.

Kendra had pictured a chance meeting between them. After all this time, seeing him would be so much different than when she was a hormonal teenager. They would recognize each other and smile in remembrance of foolish youth. Perhaps they would have coffee together in a café and chat pleasantly while they caught up on each other's lives. Maybe she would be a little sad at their parting, but she would be able to put the past to rest and know that she had moved on.

She had never expected to be jolted by the same intense desire he had aroused in her back then. And she had certainly never expected to see that same desire flare in his dark eyes again.

The years had made him even more attractive, if that was possible. Quite simply, he looked like a million bucks. He was wearing a sharp business suit, and he was impeccably groomed. His hair was shorter than before, more clean-cut and office appropriate. All traces of boyishness had faded from his features, and he was now very much a man.

"Do you guys know each other?"

It was only when she spoke that Kendra became aware of Kelly's presence beside Dominic. She remembered that she was still in her workplace and tried to regain her professional demeanor.

"We went to high school together," Dominic answered the perky receptionist.

"Wow, small world, huh? You guys should catch up and stuff."

Fortunately, Kendra was long past the blushing phase of her life, or she would have flushed in embarrassment at Kelly's obvious scheme to hook them up. "I'm sure that Mr. Miller—"

"I was just about to ask you to dinner," Dominic interrupted her awkward attempt at formality.

"I don't get off work until—"

Kelly was the one to interrupt her this time. "C'mon, Kendra. You're always the last one to leave, and you hardly ever take a lunch. Nobody's going to hold it against you if you leave early this one time."

"I'm glad I caught you," Mr. Emery said as he approached them. "You forgot your briefcase."

"Did I?" Dominic asked casually. "Good thing I stopped to say hello to Miss Davis, or I would have had to turn around in rush hour traffic and come back for it."

"Do you know Miss Davis?" Mr. Emery enquired in surprise.

"We were high school classmates," Dominic explained. "I was just trying to convince her to have dinner with me. It seems she's too dedicated to leave a minute before quitting time."

"If anyone's earned it, she has. Miss Davis, take a break and go enjoy yourself. It'll refresh your mind. We don't want our employees dropping from exhaustion."

With one of the senior partners urging her out the door,

Kendra had no choice but to leave with Dominic. She gave him a sideways glance after they were out of earshot. "Leaving your briefcase. Really?"

He smiled. "I thought I might need a little help convincing you."

She couldn't help smiling back. "How did you manage to charm Emery anyway?"

"I think it has something to do with the company I work for," he said with a hint of his old smirk.

She laughed. "Okay, spit it out. I can see you're dying to brag about it."

"Me? Brag? Okay, I'll tell you since you insist. Ever heard of the Dominiko Corporation?"

"You lucky bastard," Kendra swore. "I always knew you'd get everything you wanted."

"Well, I'm not CEO yet," he said, making her roll her eyes. "Anyway, it looks like you're doing pretty well for yourself too, working for one of the biggest law firms in Chicago."

"Yeah, I was lucky to get my foot in the door."

He looked at her curiously because of her dour tone. Kendra looked away, however, so he hailed a cab. He held the door open for her, and she scooted over so he wouldn't have to go around to the other side.

"Lady's choice," Dominic offered. "Where do you want to go?"

"I don't know," she replied. "Where do you live?"

It took Dominic only seconds to recover from the obvious implication of her words. The driver's laugh was cut short by his terse recital of his address. They rode in tense silence until they arrived at Dominic's apartment building.

"Enjoy your evening," the driver dared to say after he already got his tip.

"Thanks, we will," Kendra answered.

Her blood hummed with desire as Dominic escorted her

into the building. She waited impatiently in the elevator, which was unfortunately not empty of other people. Dominic also watched the numbers until they stopped on the seventh floor. There was nobody in the hallway, but he didn't break his stride until he halted in front of his door.

Only after they were inside with the door bolted did he turn his full attention on Kendra. He locked his smoldering gaze on her before closing the short distance between them. She moaned as he plundered her mouth with a savage kiss. Her hands were all over him, greedy to touch him again after being denied contact for so long.

They left a trail of clothes on the floor during their passionate journey to his bedroom. He settled between her legs on the bed and began to kiss his way down her body, but she grabbed his head and made him look at her.

"I need you now," she demanded in near desperation.

He slipped a finger inside her to make sure that she was ready and inhaled sharply at finding her so wet. Dominic reached over and yanked open the nightstand drawer to grab a box of condoms. Digging one out, he flung the rest on the floor and ripped open the foil packet to put it on. He groaned as he entered her and began to slowly thrust within her. Kendra wanted more, and she hooked her feet over his shoulders so he could thrust deeper.

"Yes," she cried. "Oh yes!"

"God, I've missed you," Dominic rasped as he watched her take pleasure in what he was doing to her.

Kendra broke eye contact as she began to moan in abandon. Her hands scrabbled for purchase and gripped the sheet in tight fistfuls as her head came up off the pillow during her frenzied climb to the peak. She lost control of what she was saying in those final, wild moments.

"Oh, please yes. I want it. Please, Dominic. Yes!"

"That's it sweetheart," he urged. "Come for me, Kendra."

She came with a scream and fell back on the pillow as he continued to move within her. Instead of the furious thrusting that would follow her orgasm during their teenage trysts, Dominic drew out his pleasure as he luxuriated in the feel of her.

"Look at me," he commanded roughly. "See what you do to me?"

She opened her eyes and gazed at the heated, intensely sexual expression on his face. He ran his hands up her legs as his dark eyes continued to burn into hers. "Soon as I saw you."

His speech began to fracture as his breath hitched. "Wanted…oh fuck yeah." He moaned. "Oh, so good."

He lost control and increased the speed of his thrusts until he moaned long and low with his release.

Dominic collapsed on the bed beside her as he breathed heavily.

As soon as she lost contact with his body, Kendra realized the rashness of her actions. The first thing she had done after not seeing him for seven years was jump straight into bed with him. She didn't even know anything about him. He could be married for all she knew. Not to mention that he was a client, for fuck's sake.

"I still owe you a dinner," he said lazily.

Kendra shot out of bed and began searching for her clothes.

"I guess you're really hungry," he teased as he stood up. "Let me just clean up, and—"

"This was a mistake." She pulled on her panties and retrieved her bra. "Just call me a cab, and I'll go home."

"It was no mistake," he insisted angrily. "You wanted it just as much as I did."

"Well, I can see that you haven't changed." She struggled with the clasp on her bra. "You still have an ego the size of Texas."

He came up behind her and hooked her bra for her. "You

haven't grown up at all. Have you, Kendra? As soon as I scratch that itch for you, your claws come out to tear me to shreds."

"I was fine without you," she yelled and stomped out into the hallway to find her skirt. "I didn't need you to scratch anything."

"Is that right?" Dominic drawled as he leaned against a wall and watched her shimmy into her skirt. "That's why you opted to skip dinner in favor of some afternoon delight."

"I was horny," she allowed. "You just happened to be there. Anyone with the right equipment could have done the job. It didn't have to be you."

"I see," he said coldly. "Glad I could be of service." He went into the bathroom and slammed the door.

Kendra went into the living room to pick the rest of her clothes up off the floor. She looked around in irritation, noticing for the first time how nice his apartment was. She looked up the number for the cab company on her phone and called for a taxi. Dominic was dressed in casual clothes when he joined her in the living room.

"Do you live here alone?" Kendra asked.

He answered her with an expression she couldn't pinpoint. "Yes, alone."

"How the hell does a twenty-five-year-old afford a place like this?" She was practically glaring at him now.

"I made some good investments," he told her.

"Of course you did," she groused. "Everything works out the way you want."

"So, you're angry with me because I've been successful. Would it have made you happy to see me fail?"

"It would have made me happy not to see you at all," she spat at him.

"I'm sorry I bothered you. It won't happen again." He walked to the door. "I'll see you to your cab."

"That's not necessary," she began.

"It is necessary," he ground out. "I don't slam the door shut in women's faces after I fuck them."

He held the door open, and Kendra swept out of his apartment. They left the same way they had arrived—in complete silence—but there was a much different tension between them this time.

It was still light out as they stepped out of the building. Dominic followed her to the cab when it arrived, and said goodbye to her after she gave her address to the driver. She replied with a curt goodbye and looked straight ahead as the taxi pulled away and left Dominic standing beside the curb and watching her departure.

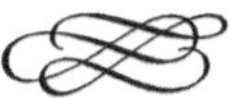

CHAPTER 16

Caroline was the only one who would understand her predicament. Samantha would just urge her to keep hooking up with Dominic if she knew about it. Kendra had already had to lie through her teeth all week at work, because Kelly was dying to know all about her dinner with their hot new client. Since she couldn't admit the truth, she'd had to describe their nonexistent dining experience at a fancy restaurant. Then she'd had to make up details about his life since high school, because they had supposedly spent their evening catching up. She'd tried to keep things as general as possible, but Kelly was hooked on every false word.

"When are you going out again?" she asked.

"We're not," Kendra answered. "It was nice to catch up, but it's not like we were best friends in high school or anything." She hoped that downplaying their relationship would make Kelly lose interest in it.

"But you said that he's single," Kelly reminded her.

Kendra had based this guess on their previous conversations in high school. She recalled his insistence that marriage wasn't for him. "Yeah, so?"

"You're single too. He obviously likes you if he asked you out."

The only reason she was even having this conversation with Kelly was because they weren't at the office. Kendra had decided that it was better to accept the receptionist's invitation to go out for lunch than to have her pestering her about Dominic at work.

"He was just being polite. You know, like when you see someone at a school reunion."

"It didn't seem like that to me," Kelly said dubiously. "I mean, he was totally checking you out."

Kendra couldn't bring herself to repeat her line about not dating clients after what she had done with Dominic that day. "I'm not looking for a relationship right now." That was the truth at least.

"That's when it's most likely to happen—when you're not looking. Fate just brings someone into your life."

Oh brother, Kendra thought. This girl had never gotten past the high school mindset. "How about you?" She shifted the focus onto Kelly. "Are you dating anyone?"

"Yes," she said happily. "He was my boss where I worked before. That's what I mean about fate bringing someone into your life. I didn't know it would turn out to be my boss."

Kendra frowned. "Isn't it against company policy for a supervisor to date an employee?"

Kelly nodded. "That's why I quit my job. So we could be together."

Kendra was appalled by this situation. "You made a big sacrifice for him."

"That's what you do when you love someone. I can replace my job, but I can't replace him."

"What did *he* do for *you*?" Kendra countered. "It seems like you're the one who had to change your life for him."

"It didn't make sense for him to quit," Kelly explained. "He makes a lot more money than I do. Anyway, I want to be a stay-at-home mom after we get married."

If you get married, Kendra thought. She didn't voice her doubt, because it wouldn't make any difference. Kelly had already made her choice. In any case, there was no way to predict the outcome. Her own sister was a stay-at-home mom, and she seemed surprisingly happy.

Kendra had never expected Veronica to be able to settle down like that. The girl had flunked out of college because of her excessive partying. Then she had gotten a job as a flight attendant, which Kendra thought was actually the perfect job for her on-the-go sister. She had met her husband while working a flight from California to Hawaii. Who knew that her little sister would get married and have kids before her?

"You should give Dominic a chance," Kelly suddenly said.

I already gave him a chance, and he dumped me. Kendra shook her head, both to Kelly's comment and to clear her head of such thoughts. "I'm happy with my life the way it is."

She waited until Friday night when Samantha went out before she called Caroline to vent. It was a relief to spill her guts to someone. "I can't believe I did that!"

"So, things are just as hot and heavy between you as they always were," Caroline said in an excited tone that echoed Kelly's view on the situation.

"Did you hear me? I had a one-night stand with a client."

"He's your ex-boyfriend, Kendra. It's a little different than seducing a client."

"This isn't high school anymore," Kendra chided her. "We're talking about my job."

"Since the senior partner gave you his blessing, I don't think your job's in jeopardy," Caroline said. "What's this really about, Kendra?"

She was quiet for a moment as she thought back on things

that she had left behind in her youth. "It was hard when it ended. I don't want to go through that again."

"I know it's scary, but he obviously still has feelings for you if—"

"He doesn't have feelings," she interrupted Caroline vehemently. "He has sex. That's it. Yeah, I'll admit it's damn good sex, but that's all it is."

Caroline sighed. "So, what are you going to do?"

"Nothing. It's already done. Now I just have to hope that he doesn't approach me at work again."

That workweek ended without another sighting of Dominic, and Kendra was glad it was over. She was looking forward to collapsing in bed after her shower. Her weariness evaporated in an instant when she entered her apartment and found Dominic seated on her couch with Samantha.

"Hey girlfriend," Samantha greeted her. "Why didn't you tell me that you have a date tonight?"

Unfortunately, her death glare seemed to be having no effect on Dominic. The sneaky bastard was still alive and smirking at her. "What are you doing here?" Kendra asked through gritted teeth.

"Since I gave you a tour of my apartment last time, I thought it was only fair that you return the favor."

His meaning was not lost on Samantha. "Well," she said brightly. "Now that you're here to keep him company, I'll go get ready. I'm meeting some friends pretty soon."

Kendra knew that was a lie. It was only seven-thirty, and nobody went out before ten on a Saturday night. "No, don't—"

"Don't wanna be late," Samantha talked over her. "Excuse me." She hurried off to her room.

"Get out," Kendra hissed, turning on Dominic.

He didn't move from his comfortable position on the couch. "I just had a very enlightening conversation with your roommate."

"You said that you wouldn't bother me again," Kendra reminded him angrily.

"We both lied. Didn't we?"

"I didn't," she began.

"What about that bullshit you told me after we had sex?" Dominic demanded.

"Keep your voice down!" She glanced reflexively toward Samantha's closed door.

"According to your roommate, you haven't been on any dates since you broke up with your boyfriend five months ago."

"That's none of your business," she said in a loud whisper.

He continued to speak in a normal volume. "You're an adult now. Nobody's going to be shocked if you have sex."

"I don't want to broadcast my personal life to—"

"The person who lives with you," he finished for her. "Yet you had no problem telling me that any cock will do for you."

"Oh, did I offend your strict moral code?" She had forgotten to keep lowering her voice as she argued with him. "I guess it's only acceptable for guys to sleep around."

"I'm not concerned with how many guys you've been with, only that you lied about why you were with me. You could have picked up any guy if you were just horny. You chose me, because you wanted me."

"Here we go again with your pathetic need for sexual reassurance. What's the matter, Dominic? Losing your touch?" Kendra taunted.

He caught her off guard when he suddenly grabbed her and pulled her onto his lap. "You seem to like my touch just fine sweetheart."

"Let go." She struggled against his iron hold on her. He obviously still worked out, judging by his strong muscles.

His arms were firmly wrapped around her as she squirmed against him. She got goosebumps as he spoke into her ear. "Keep that up, and we won't make it off this couch."

"You can't do this," she protested.

"Do what?" His voice dropped lower. "Turn you on?"

Samantha hurried out of her room, apparently haven gotten ready in record time. "Have fun you two. No, don't get up," she said as Kendra opened her mouth to say something.

"Already am," Dominic said, but she was at the door and didn't hear his innuendo.

Kendra fumed silently after Samantha closed the door, and they were left alone in the apartment.

"Now, about that tour," Dominic rumbled in her ear.

CHAPTER 17

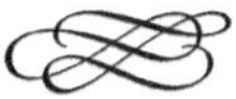

*D*ominic held firmly to her waist with one arm while his other hand lifted her skirt to expose her thighs. His fingers lightly caressed her leg as he spoke into her ear. "I've been thinking about you all week. Wanting to touch you."

His hand moved ever so slowly up her thigh, and Kendra waited in delicious anticipation for him to reach her most sensitive spot. He only brushed his fingers over her panties with the barest touch, but she moaned and threw her head back against his shoulder.

He slid his hand teasingly up her other thigh. "Do you want me to touch you?"

"Yes," she answered in mindless arousal.

"Are you sure you're not just horny?" Dominic asked.

They sat motionless until Kendra opened her eyes. She then realized that he had placed his hands down on the couch, and she was sitting on his lap of her own volition with her legs open in invitation to him.

Feeling a mixture of anger and embarrassment, along with an unfulfilled ache between her legs, she stood up and smoothed down her skirt. "So, you came here to rub it in. Real mature, Dominic."

"Actually, I came here to take you out to that dinner we didn't get to have last time. I am, of course, open to other suggestions," he ended smoothly.

"Oh, I have a few suggestions for you alright." Kendra glared at him. "How did you get in here, anyway?" She knew that nobody could get into the building without a key or being buzzed in by a resident.

"It wasn't easy," he confided. "You must really spend all of your time at work. Do you know that most of the people in this building don't even know you exist? Luckily, Samantha came along and was thrilled to meet your cousin. Of course, I had to tell her who I really was after she offered to—keep me entertained, shall we say—until you got home."

As if he didn't already have a big enough ego, Kendra thought in annoyance. "I'm surprised you didn't take her up on her offer."

"That would preclude me from having sex with you again." His dark eyes burned with an inner fire as he looked at her. "I very much want to have more sex with you, Kendra."

How the hell was she supposed to think rationally with him looking at her that way? "That was a one-time thing. I'd appreciate it if you'd—"

"It's never been a one-time thing with us." He stood up in fervent denial of her statement. "Our attraction hasn't faded even after all these years. I know you feel it too."

"So, what now?" Kendra asked bitterly. "I should just let you fuck me until you get tired of me again?"

"I never got tired of you," he said. "I just knew that a long-distance relationship wasn't going to work."

"You never even tried! You just walked away like it meant nothing to you, the way you always do. Well, I'm telling you to keep walking." She was so agitated that she spun away from him and stormed into her room.

He stopped her from slamming the door shut in his face. "That's what this is all about, isn't it? You're still hung up on what happened in high school."

"Oh, you mean the fact that you used me and dumped me? Why would I be upset about that?" She gave up on trying to close the door and flounced over to her bed.

He came in and stood looking down at her. "I didn't use you, Kendra. I'll admit that I was a player in high school, but I had a real relationship with you. We did all the things any other couple did."

"You think because you took me to prom, you're absolved of all responsibility for breaking my heart?"

She realized what she had just admitted to him and dropped her gaze into her lap. "Just go," she pleaded.

He sank down to crouch in front of her and gently lift her face to look at him. "I'm sorry. I didn't know you felt that way."

"Forget it," she said. "It's in the past."

"I can't forget it," he insisted. "I haven't ever been able to forget about you."

"What are you saying?" Kendra asked.

"I'm saying that things between us aren't finished," he answered as his thumb stroked her chin.

"And when they are?" She spoke softly. "What then?"

"I don't know," he replied honestly. "I just know that I want to be with you. Nobody knows how long any relationship will last, but I know that's what I want with you."

She knew that it would end in heartache again, but she couldn't fight her feelings. "I want to be with you too."

Dominic smiled and leaned in to kiss her. They ended up making out on her bed before he pulled away. "Slow down. Now that I know I have you, I want to take my time with you."

He took a moment to appreciate the lustful look on her face.

"Hold that thought for later. I want to take you out to dinner first."

"Why'd you kick Samantha out if all you wanted to do was go out to dinner?" Kendra grumbled.

"It's not my fault that she assumed I was here to seduce you." He grinned at her frustration at being left hot and bothered. "You women with your dirty minds."

She threw a pillow at him. "Get out and let me get ready then."

"I thought you were ready," he answered cheekily as his eyes dropped to her exposed panties.

He laughed when she struggled to pull down her skirt. "Okay, I'll let you get dressed in private." His eyes moved back to her face. "The real fun is in undressing you."

He was at her bedroom door before he turned back. "Oh, and bring a change of clothes with you. I want you to sleep over at my place."

"We'll have to stop back here first. I can't take a change of clothes with me to the restaurant."

"We're going in my car," he informed her. "Bring what you need with you."

"Okay. Let's see, I'll need my nightgown too."

"No," he said with a sinful stare that made her catch her breath. "You won't."

CHAPTER 18

Dominic smiled in approval when Kendra emerged from her room wearing a simple blue silk dress. It was the same dress she had been wearing when Craig proposed to her, but he didn't need to know that.

They left the apartment and went down to where Dominic had parked his car. It was a Cadilac, but it looked more sporty than luxurious. Still, they were definitely traveling in style. The boy had come a long way since high school. He set her overnight bag in the backseat and opened the passenger door for her. She found herself remembering their first date all those years ago.

"What are you smiling about?" Dominic asked as he sat down in the driver's seat.

"Just thinking about the last time you hijacked me into going out to dinner with you."

"Yeah, Rosewood." He turned the key in the ignition, and the car purred to life.

Kendra was stunned. "You remember the name of the restaurant?"

"It was my first date with you and my birthday. Of course I remember. We went to dinner and dancing under the stars," he said before pulling away from the curb.

She didn't know what to make of his detailed memory of that evening. Kendra had been sure that he had forgotten most of what had transpired between them back then. For her, it was still the most romantic thing that had ever happened to her. Even her marriage proposal hadn't outdone that memory.

Kendra suddenly realized that she wouldn't be here with Dominic right now if she had become engaged to Craig.

"Have you ever proposed to anyone?" That wasn't the question she had planned to lead with, but she supposed they needed to begin somewhere with catching up on each other's lives.

"No, it never got that serious with anyone. How about you?" Dominic asked.

"I thought I would marry my boyfriend, but then when he asked me…"

"You were afraid of making such a huge commitment," he finished for her.

"I wasn't afraid," she explained. "I just didn't want to get married. I had no desire to take that next step."

"How long were you together?"

"Since my second year of college. I met him right after Adam broke up with Caroline." She then gave him a brief explanation about Adam wanting to see other people before launching into the story of how she had met Craig.

Her dorm roommate had finally badgered her into attending a frat party. Kendra hadn't expected to enjoy herself there, but Craig was so different from many of his obnoxious fraternity brothers. He had remained a gentleman in the midst of all the debauchery going on around them. When he asked for her number at the end of the night, she had happily given it to him.

"Smart guy," Dominic commented. "He could tell right away

that taking it slow was the only way to get a date with you. It took me a lot longer to figure that out."

"We sure didn't take it slow this time," she said ruefully.

"That's only because you can't control yourself around me," he teased. "I was willing to wait."

"If you want to wait, I can easily arrange that for you," she huffed.

"That's an empty threat if I ever heard one," he said with a sly glance at her. "I can make you wet just by talking to you."

"You're so full of yourself," she laughed.

"Has anyone found your G-spot?"

She immediately grew uncomfortable with the conversation. "Uh, that's not—"

"I can tell that the answer is no. Don't worry sweetheart. I'll find it tonight," he promised her. "First, I'm going to stimulate it with my fingers while I lick your clit. I'll bring you right to the brink that way. Then, when you're primed for it, I'm going to bend you over the arm of the couch and take you from behind. It's the perfect height and position for me to hit your sweet spot."

"Can we please talk about something else?" Kendra asked in a tight voice.

"What's wrong?" Dominic taunted. "Getting too aroused?"

She reached over and boldly placed her hand over the bulge in his pants. "I'm not the only one."

"You're right," he conceded. "We'll never make it to the restaurant if we keep this up."

"I like the sound of that," she purred and began to squeeze him.

"Kendra," he groaned.

"I can't focus on any damn dinner," she growled. "Take me to your place right now."

"Oh fuck," he swore as he felt her slip her hand beneath the waistband of his pants. "You're gonna make me crash the car."

"What's the matter, Dominic? Getting too turned on?" Kendra mimicked.

She began to caress him through his underwear. "You better find a place to pull over if you can't drive."

"You'll pay for this," he warned in a ragged voice while she slid her hand into his underwear to grasp him firmly.

She kept up her ministrations as he pulled into a parking garage and opened the window to take the ticket from the automated machine. "Just let me find a spot," he pleaded desperately as she freed him from his underwear.

It excited her to keep him on edge this way while he was forced to drive up a couple of floors to find an empty spot. He tensely gripped the wheel while taking shallow breaths as she moved her hand up and down him. The occasional moan that escaped his clenched jaw added to her heady feeling of power over him.

"Did I mention that I'm not wearing any panties?" Kendra cooed.

He rounded the corner and shot the car into the first empty spot he found, slamming it into park with an animalistic growl. Her hand lost its grip on him as his seat slid all the way back at the same time that his seatbelt snapped violently back to the unbuckled position. In the next instant, he dug through his pocket and found a condom which he managed to put on with lightning-fast speed before he released Kendra's seatbelt and pulled her roughly from her own seat.

"What are you doing?" She balanced awkwardly on his lap as he bunched her dress up to reveal that she was indeed not wearing panties.

"Did you think you were just going to give me a hand job?" He grabbed her hips to position her over him. "I hope you're ready."

"Someone might see us," she protested.

"That didn't concern you before. You're lucky I'm letting you keep your dress on."

He circumvented her retort by impaling her on top of him. She slid easily down on him due to how wet she was from all their physical and mental foreplay. His bruising kiss left her breathless, and she suspected that his almost painful hold on her hips would leave marks. She no longer cared if anyone saw them as she took over the pace he had set by grinding her up and down on him, and she rode him hard.

He grunted with the strain but was unable to hold back his release. Seeing the look on his face as he came sent her over the edge right after him. She sat panting on top of him until she heard a car start up somewhere in the vicinity.

Then she scrambled back to her seat, much to Dominic's amusement. His gruff laugh made her scowl at him.

"Your sense of modesty is delightfully flexible," he told her while he flung the condom out the window.

"That's disgusting!"

He shrugged. "What was I supposed to do with it?"

She looked around his spotless car. "You should have a trash bag in here."

"Sorry. I didn't know that I was going to be having sex in my car." His smirk showed that he wasn't sorry at all.

"Let's just get out of here," she said.

"Are you sure that you can make it to my apartment now?" Dominic taunted her. "I wouldn't want to endanger other motorists' lives again."

"Oh, shut up," she grumbled.

Kendra perked up when she saw a fast-food restaurant coming into view. "I'm hungry. Stop at that drive thru."

He chuckled. "You're a really cheap date."

"You'll be paying for those words next time," she warned him. "I'm going to pick the most expensive restaurant in town."

"It doesn't matter. We'll never get there anyway."

He laughed at the expression on her face. "C'mon, I'll buy you a happy meal."

Kendra crossed her arms and looked haughtily away from him. "I don't think I'll be talking to you anymore tonight."

"That's alright sweetheart," he said. "We don't have to talk."

CHAPTER 19

$\mathcal{A}$ powerful orgasm unlike any she had ever experienced before overwhelmed her entire body. She was sprawled over the arm of Dominic's couch while he penetrated her from behind. Kendra would have felt some trepidation about getting into this position if Dominic hadn't overcome her inhibitions by arousing her so skillfully with his fingers and tongue. The incredible feeling of having two pleasure spots stimulated at the same time drove her to a state of complete submission to her desire.

True to his word, he had found the G-spot she had doubted actually existed. He had inserted two fingers into her while he licked her clit. Then he'd curled those fingers forward to press on a point that had caused pressure to build inside her as well as on the spot he was working with his tongue. She had whimpered when he stopped his ministrations and withdrew his fingers, because she had been on the verge of release.

He had directed her to bend over the couch, and she had wantonly obeyed in order to entice him to continue what he was doing to her. Dominic had somehow managed to hit the same spot as he thrust into her.

This type of orgasm suffused her whole body with a sense of euphoria. She was only dimly aware of him continuing to thrust within her until he came. Exhaustion left her incapable of moving.

Dominic picked her up and carried her to his bedroom. "It takes a lot out of you the first time it happens." He gently set her down on the bed and got in beside her.

Kendra drifted off to sleep against the comfort of his warm body and didn't stir until morning. She woke up alone, but she smelled bacon cooking. After getting dressed in the sweatpants and t-shirt she had packed in her overnight bag, she went to find Dominic in the kitchen.

"Good morning," he greeted her. "Why'd you put on clothes?"

"Good morning." She smiled at him. "I can't walk around naked."

"Why not? There's nobody here but us. I now know that waking up with you naked in my bed is the best way to wake up. It then stands to reason that having you naked in the kitchen is the best way to eat breakfast."

She laughed. "Why should I be naked if you're not?"

"Because you're much more fun to look at," he said.

"You're right. Who would want to see you naked?" Kendra teased.

"There was this girl once who fantasized about hiding in my closet to watch me undress. After she got a good long look, I would then catch her naked in my bed and proceed to ravish her."

"That wasn't a fantasy, it was a dream. Hence the weird shift from the closet to the bed," she explained. "I can't believe you remember that. You don't still have my diary, do you?"

"Of course I do. I told you that was the only memento I wanted to keep from high school." He took hold of the hem of her t-shirt and began to lift it. "I just need a little peek."

He frowned as he exposed her cleavage. "A bra too? That's going too far."

The sound of knocking startled her but only made Dominic exclaim in exasperation. "Not now."

Kendra followed him to the door and watched him open it to reveal a blond little boy. "I'm sorry, Timmy, but—"

"Who's that?" Timmy interrupted.

"This is Kendra," Dominic introduced her.

"Does she like to play bad guys too?" Timmy slipped past Dominic. "Ooh, bacon!"

"Would you like some?" Kendra asked, ignoring Dominic's scowl.

"Yeah, and then we can play bad guys," Timmy declared.

Dominic trailed behind them as Kendra asked Timmy how he liked his eggs.

"Scrambled," Dominic answered for him. "I'll make them. He likes some cheddar cheese thrown in. How do you want yours?"

Kendra watched how easy and natural Dominic's interaction was with Timmy. She had never expected him to be so comfortable with a kid. It made her think that it was a shame he didn't want kids of his own, because he appeared to be so good with them. Timmy obviously idolized him. His face fell when Dominic told him that they couldn't play after breakfast.

"I have a guest right now," he explained. "We can play next time."

"She can play too," Timmy suggested.

"Yeah," Kendra agreed. "I like to play games."

"We'll play next time. Go home now. We've got work to do." He escorted Timmy to the door and closed it firmly behind him.

"Maybe we should have walked him home," she fretted.

"He'll be fine. He lives right down the hall," Dominic told her.

"You could have let him stay. I didn't mind."

"I do." He stepped forward to lift her shirt up again. "I can't get you naked with him here." He pulled her shirt over her head. "These clothes have been on long enough."

Dominic suddenly leaned down to attach his mouth to her nipple right through the lacy fabric of her bra, and Kendra couldn't argue with his logic.

CHAPTER 20

"You wore that on your date?"

These were the first words out of Samantha's mouth when Dominic left after taking Kendra back to her apartment Sunday evening. She regarded Kendra's sweatpants and t-shirt combination with something bordering on horror. "You got yourself a fine man like Dominic, and you're wearing *that*?"

Kendra looked down at herself and shrugged. Her less than sexy outfit sure hadn't cooled Dominic's ardor. They'd had sex twice that day. The first time had been right after breakfast, and the second time had taken place in the shower a couple hours later. He'd stepped into the stall with her just after she'd soaped herself up, and he'd gotten her into a different kind of lather.

Having sex in the shower was another fantasy she'd never fulfilled until then. She was doing a lot of things with Dominic that she'd never done with anyone else. She was used to only having sex in bed, but he told her that he wanted to try out every room in his apartment with her.

Kendra pulled her thoughts back to the present. "I wore a dress out to dinner yesterday." She motioned to her overnight bag on the floor. No need to tell her roommate that they'd never made it to the restaurant.

"Okay, so today was casual, but you still didn't have to wear sweatpants. You need to get yourself some sexy miniskirts for days like that," Samantha advised her.

She'd never been one to flaunt her body, but imagining the way Dominic would look at her made her reconsider. "Maybe I'll go shopping after work on Friday."

"Finally!" Samantha exclaimed in triumph. "You'll look so hot that he won't be able to keep his hands off you."

Her lips curved into a suggestive smile. "So, tell me. Is he as good as he looks?"

Kendra couldn't hide her satisfied smile as images of their torrid lovemaking sprang to mind.

"You lucky bitch," Samantha laughed. "No wonder you weren't interested in the losers I tried to hook you up with. You've got fucking great taste girlfriend."

She smiled at Kendra. "Nobody deserves it more than you, even if I am jealous. Too bad he wasn't really your cousin."

"Speaking of that, you took a big chance letting a stranger in here. He could have been a serial killer for all you knew," Kendra admonished her.

"Or he could have really been your cousin." Samantha shrugged. Then she sighed dreamily. "That man is really into you. He could have taken advantage of the situation before he told me the truth, but he was a perfect gentleman."

"Yeah, he told me about that." Kendra shook her head at Samantha's free spirit lifestyle.

"More points for him," Samantha said approvingly. "He didn't even hide that from you. You know I never would have come on to him if I knew he was yours, but it did help you see his true colors. That man is one in a million. I've never known a guy to turn down a blowjob, have you?"

Kendra had thought that she was past the point of anything

making her blush, but her cheeks flamed as she looked uncomfortably away.

"Oh honey," Samantha cried. "You can't be serious! You've never given a guy a blowjob?"

"I don't want to get into that," Kendra said.

She had meant the discussion, but Samantha mistook her meaning for the act itself. "You know how you like it when a guy goes down on you? Well, it's the same for guys. They love to get blowjobs. It can be a big turn on for the girl too."

Kendra didn't tell her that Dominic was the only guy who had ever given her oral sex. Her lovemaking with Craig had been much more pleasurable than with Caleb, and she had climaxed regularly. None of their sex had been as adventurous and wild as what she had experienced with Dominic, however. He brought out a side to her that nobody else ever had.

"Thanks," she said in order to end the conversation. "I'll keep that in mind."

"I can demonstrate it for you," Samantha offered. "I think we have a cucumber in here." She made a move as if to walk toward the kitchen.

"No! I think I, uh, will figure it out."

Samantha broke out into gales of laughter. "I was just kidding. Oh, the look on your face!"

Kendra decided that she had already gotten out of her comfort zone enough by having sex in a public garage. She would put off thinking about trying out anymore new sexual activities for the time being. Things were already moving at a fast pace. They were having sex before they'd actually gotten reacquainted. She vowed to actually make it out to dinner next time so they could talk.

The workweek passed at its usual snail's pace of mind-numbing tedium. Her job basically consisted of going through stacks of contracts to make sure they were correct. It was far removed from what she wanted to be doing with her career, but it was helping her pay down her debt. Dominic worked long hours too, but he was excited about his job. He called her every evening to see how her day was and wish her a goodnight.

"Sounds like you could use a vacation," he told her.

"Maybe in my next life," she said.

"I was thinking about finally taking that trip to Fiji. I'd like you to come with me."

Kendra tried to stop herself from imagining what it would be like to frolic in a tropical paradise with Dominic. "Thanks, but I can't afford that."

"Still worried about paying your way, I see. Since I invited you, it'll be my treat," he insisted.

"We just started dating. I can't let you do something like that. It's too much." She was thrilled that he had asked her though.

"With all the money that I'm saving on our dates, it'll pay for the trip. Please think about it, Kendra. We'll plan on four months from now. That'll give you plenty of time to give notice at work and get time off."

It sounded so tempting. "I'll think about it."

The day that she had been looking forward to all week finally arrived. Kendra wore another dress from her closet to go out to dinner, but she packed one of her new casual outfits in her overnight bag. Dominic had invited her to sleep over again Saturday night, and she had accepted. This was the part that she loved the most about their grown-up relationship. She didn't have to go home at the end of the evening the way she did when they were teens.

Determined to keep their conversation from becoming X-rated this time, Kendra led with a question about his family. "How's your dad?"

"He's good," Dominic replied.

She noticed the tension in his body language and kept silent as she waited for him to elaborate.

After a moment, he exhaled and continued. "He remarried my mother."

"That's great," she exclaimed.

"Is it? How long will it be before she breaks his heart again?"

Kendra was surprised by his unfavorable reaction. She had always thought that kids of divorced parents wished for a reconciliation between them. "Maybe she's changed."

"That's what my dad believes. He says that she's cleaned up her act and gotten sober." Dominic stared unhappily out at the road as he drove.

"How does she seem to you?" Kendra asked.

He was silent for a moment. "I haven't seen her. They got back together three years ago, and I've been avoiding going home. My dad and I still do our camping thing every summer, and I just meet him at the campground. He's tried to talk me into stopping by the house, but I flat out told him that it's not going to happen."

She saw the stubborn set of his jaw, but she broached the subject anyway. "What would it hurt just to talk to her?"

"She abandoned me when I was younger than Timmy. How could she do that?"

Kendra thought about the little boy he had been, and her heart broke for him. "Maybe it would make you feel better to confront her. You could ask her that question."

"She tried to apologize to me, but I hung up on her. There's nothing she can say to make it right. She wasn't there for me when I needed her, so I don't want her in my life now. I just hope she doesn't screw over my dad again."

"I guess that's the risk you take when you love someone," she mused.

"Yeah," he agreed.

Kendra looked at him in surprise. She distinctly remembered him telling her that he didn't believe in love. Had he changed his mind since high school? She wanted to ask him if he'd ever been in love, but he wasn't in the best mood right now.

Changing the subject seemed to be the best idea. "So, how was your college experience?"

They were still sharing college memories when they arrived at the restaurant. The place was upscale but not outrageously expensive. Kendra couldn't help but think of the last time she'd been there.

"What is it?" Dominic asked.

She was startled that he had picked up on anything. "Nothing." She smiled at him.

"Tell me," he insisted.

"This is, um, where Craig proposed to me," she admitted.

"We can go somewhere else," he offered.

"No, really, it's fine. This place probably has bad memories for him, but it doesn't bother me." She winced. "Poor Craig. He got down on one knee, and it drew attention to us. Then it was so awkward when I said no."

"Ouch," Dominic said. "That's why it's not a good idea to propose in public. Listen, seriously, I'll take you somewhere else if you want."

"And risk not getting there? We finally made it out to dinner, and I'm making up for that cheap meal you bought me last time," she teased.

"That was your choice," he reminded her. "I was all set to take you to dinner, but you couldn't keep your hands off me."

"Let me tell you a secret." She leaned in closer to him and lowered her voice. "I might not be able to keep my hands off you tonight either."

He tried to kiss her, but she scrambled out of the car. She was laughing when he caught up to her and pulled her into that kiss. "Food first," she scolded as she broke away from him.

He asked about her family after the waitress took their orders. She told him about Veronica getting married and having twins. Once she was on the subject of stay-at-home moms, she even related the story about Kelly and her former boss.

"I think she's making a big mistake. She already quit one job for him, and now she's planning to quit another one if he marries her."

"Like you said, those are the risks you take when you love someone," Dominic said.

This was the second time they were on the subject, so she ventured a question disguised as a comment. "I thought you didn't believe in love."

"I'm not sure anymore." He observed her reaction to that confession.

"That's truly astonishing, Dominic. I thought you'd always be a cynic."

"I was never a cynic," he corrected her. "Only a realist. I have to admit though, that some things can't be explained with logic."

She was dying to ask him if he'd ever been in love, but something held her back. "What made you change your mind?"

He seemed to be choosing his words carefully before he spoke again. "I guess there's no other way to explain still feeling such a strong attachment to someone after so many years of being apart."

"You mean your dad still being in love with your mom?" Kendra asked.

There was a pause before he answered. "Yeah, that's what I mean."

He was clearly not keen on talking about his parents. "So, uh, what about you? Do you still believe in love?"

"I believe in it, but I haven't found it. I guess Craig was right when he said that I wasn't in love with him. I was fond of him, and I thought that was enough. But then I just couldn't marry him after all. I don't know. Maybe I'm expecting too much," she mused.

"You're not," he told her. "Settling for less than you want will never make you happy. Anyway, I'm glad you turned him down, because it's given us a second chance."

"Me too," she admitted, suddenly shy.

"Have you been thinking about Fiji?" Dominic asked. "I'd like to make the arrangements."

She took a sip of her wine as she imagined being in paradise with him. Kendra had already found herself daydreaming about it at work. Thinking about everything in her life she had postponed in order to succeed professionally, she suddenly made her decision on a whim. "I want to go with you."

His smile was as warm as the sun upon hearing her answer. "We can both put in for the time off on Monday. I was thinking we could go for ten days. That'll give us time when we get home if we take the full two weeks of vacation."

"That sounds good," she agreed.

They continued to talk through their meal. Kendra questioned him about Timmy, and she learned that the little boy was eight years old. They had met in the hallway one day, and the kid had followed him to his door. After that, he started coming around knocking on his door and wanting to hang out. Dominic made sure that his parents were aware of the visits.

"I'm an only child too, so I know how lonely it can be. Anyway, he's a good kid."

Kendra beamed at him. "That's so nice," she gushed.

"Did you think that I can only be bad?"

His teasing smile brought out a playful response from her. "I'm just wondering how bad you can be."

He leaned closer to her and spoke low. "You're about to find out sweetheart."

The next thing she knew, she felt his hand on her knee. "I have to go to the restroom." She vacated her chair in alarm and turned to make her escape.

"I'll pay the check and be ready to go when you get back. Unless you want dessert," he offered.

Kendra half-turned toward him. "No, I'm full."

"Not yet," he said with that ever-changing smile. It now looked wickedly sinful.

She fled to the restroom, chiding herself for goading him in a public place. His threat to make her pay for what she had done to him in his car was now on her mind. She hoped that he was just bluffing and wouldn't really embarrass her in front of other people.

Even so, not knowing what to expect excited her. It made her hyperaware of his every move. She had the sense that he could pounce on her at any moment, and it heightened her anticipation of what was to come.

"You seem kind of nervous," Dominic commented after they left the restaurant. "Did you think that I was going to follow you into the restroom?"

"I never know what you're going to do," she told him.

"Remember when we had sex in the bathroom at school?" He laughed at the look on her face.

"We just made out," she corrected him. "We didn't go all the way."

He waited until they were seated in his car before continuing the conversation. "Oh yeah. That was only in my imagination afterwards when I masturbated while thinking about it."

She primly smoothed down her dress over her knees while it secretly aroused her to know that he thought about her while touching himself. "Do you still do that?"

"Think about you while I masturbate?" He started the car and pulled out of the parking space. "Of course. Having sex with you only on the weekend is not enough." He glanced at her. "Do you think about me while you masturbate?"

Kendra had never talked with anyone about masturbation before. She would have been embarrassed to admit that she sometimes pleasured herself. It felt like a dirty, shameful secret. Going a long time between boyfriends was only part of the reason she turned to solo orgasms. Her high sex drive had not been satisfied with the amount of sex her busy boyfriend had been able to provide for her. Being busy herself, she also didn't always feel like going through the whole production of having sex. It was quicker and easier to take care of it herself.

"I fantasize about you a lot," she said.

Dominic immediately picked up on her discomfort about this subject and took perverse pleasure in it. "Do you remember when I told you you'd pay for that stunt you pulled last weekend?"

She felt safer now that they were on the way to his apartment. "Yes, but I already did. I had sex with you in a public garage."

"That was something that you chose to do when you initiated sex in my car. Yes, Kendra," he cut off her protest. "When you won't let go of my cock, you're asking for sex. Now for payback, I get to make you do something that makes you uncomfortable. So, I want to watch you play with yourself until we get to my place. If you come, then you've paid me back."

Kendra felt herself getting wet as she imagined doing something so naughty. "You can't watch me. You have to drive."

"Don't worry. If I didn't crash the car with you trying to jerk me off, I won't now. I'll be able to watch the road too."

She couldn't bring herself to break this taboo. Kendra didn't even know if she could do that in front of him behind closed doors, let alone in his car. "I can't."

"C'mon. You don't even have to expose yourself. Just put your hand inside your panties and touch yourself," he coaxed.

"I can't do that in front of anyone else. I just can't." She was embarrassed even about admitting that much to him. Now he knew that she masturbated.

"Then I'll just have to think of another way to get even with you," he threatened.

She was waiting for him to do something wild, but it didn't

happen. Kendra's mouth went dry when they got in the elevator alone. She half-expected him to have sex with her right there like she had seen in the movies. Once they were in his apartment, she decided that he had just been playing mind games with her. It had certainly been effective, because she was in a heightened state of arousal.

"Yeah," he said, pushing her against the door and checking inside her panties, "that turned you on. Just imagine how turned on you'd be if you actually did it."

He took her hand and put it between her legs. "Show me. I want to watch you touch yourself."

His hoarse voice revealed to her how much the thought of that turned him on, but she still couldn't do it. "I'm sorry, Dominic. I can't."

He let it go for the time being and led her to his bedroom. They began to kiss and undress each other. Kendra ended up on top again, but she took it slow this time to prolong her pleasure. She leaned back with her hands gripping his thighs as she rocked her body into him. They snuggled together afterwards and drifted off to sleep in blissful contentment.

She awoke before him this time and snuck off to the bathroom. Rummaging quietly in her overnight bag, she was able to get dressed without waking him. He found her later cooking breakfast in the kitchen.

"I thought I smelled…"

She turned to see him checking her out. "You like?" She did a little curtsy.

"That's a sexy skirt." He leered at her. "I was going to say that you better be naked this time, but I think I'm going to allow the skirt." He lifted it to see what was underneath. "These panties have to go, however."

"Those are brand new," she protested. "I just bought them yesterday."

"Completely unnecessary," he stated. "You have to learn to make better investments."

"I bought this skirt yesterday too," she informed him.

"A much wiser choice." He moved his hand beneath it to grab her rear. "I like the silky material, but your skin feels much better."

That's when they were interrupted by knocking on the door. "See?" Kendra told him. "You don't always have the best advice. What would I do now in a skirt this short without any underwear?"

"Do you really need me to answer that question?" He chuckled at the look she gave him. "Of course, we wouldn't answer the door if we were doing that."

"Coming," Kendra yelled as the knocking continued.

"Oh, you will be later," Dominic promised before going to answer the door.

Timmy had breakfast with them again. He remembered Kendra and treated her like a buddy. Despite Dominic's impatience, she agreed to play bad guys with the little boy. He ran excitedly toward Dominic's office.

Kendra avoided looking at the leather couch in there, because it was the one they had used for sex last weekend. Timmy walked over to the desk and pulled out a Monopoly game and two Nerf guns from one of the drawers.

Kendra stared at the next two items he found in there. "I'm afraid to ask." She knew that the child wouldn't know what they were talking about.

Dominic picked up one pair of handcuffs. "They're from my Houdini phase."

She wasn't sure if she believed that story. "You had a Houdini phase?"

"I mastered the trick of escaping handcuffs," he confirmed.

"Seriously, you can get out of those? How?"

A mysterious smile played over his lips. "A magician never reveals his secrets."

"C'mon guys," Timmy said. "Let's play. I'm the bad guy, and Dominic's the cop." He motioned for Kendra to approach him. "You sit here and work in the bank."

She sat down in the chair and looked at the stacks of play money that Timmy had arranged on the desk. Dominic had to leave the room so Timmy could rob her. He then handcuffed each of her wrists to the arms of the chair with a separate pair of handcuffs. His skill and assurance with them made it obvious that he had handled them many times before.

She had been sure that they were magician's props, but they felt real. Kendra couldn't find the trick to opening them, and she wondered how Dominic got out of them. He stormed into the room and ordered Timmy to drop his weapon. They began to unload their Nerf guns on each other while Timmy took cover behind Kendra.

Some of the bullets hit her. "Hey, you're shooting the hostage!"

"Sorry," Dominic said. "Friendly fire."

"You're wearing a bullet-proof vest," Timmy improvised.

Dominic was the one who heard the knocking on the door. Timmy naturally followed him to satisfy his curiosity. Kendra could hear the murmur of voices, but only Timmy's was loud enough to distinguish exactly what he was saying. She heard him shouting that they were playing bad guys, and that he didn't want to go. It was obviously to no avail, because Dominic returned without him.

"His grandma has arrived, and he has to go visit with her," he explained.

Kendra waited expectantly for him to release her, but he only stood there silently observing her before he spoke. "Well, isn't this a tantalizing predicament."

The wicked gleam in his eyes matched the very wicked smile that suddenly appeared on his face.

Her heart began to pound, but she tried not to show her unease at the thought of him being into freaky stuff. She had never experimented with anything remotely kinky. "Let me go."

Her voice quavered slightly, and his smile seemed to become even more dangerous.

He placed his hands on the desk and leaned in to look more closely at her. "I think this is the perfect way to get even with you for last week. You're completely at my mercy now."

"Dominic, I mean it. Let me go." She sounded about as forceful as a mouse, and she knew that her eyes were wide as saucers.

He straightened up and walked toward her with deliberate, measured steps. She shrank back into the chair as her heart thundered in her chest. He slowly rolled the chair back and spun her toward him. "I will after."

"After what?" Kendra asked fearfully.

His dark eyes roamed slowly down her body before he answered. "After I make you come."

"You don't need to have me in handcuffs to make me come," she said breathlessly. He had scared her into being short of breath.

"This is how I'll get my revenge. I can really take my time with you now."

He watched her expression change to one of relief. "I can see that you think you're getting off easy, but I know how impatient you are when you want something."

This mind game had really been going too far. "You scared the hell out of me, you jackass!"

"Why? Did you think I was going to keep you chained up as my sex slave?" He laughed as color crept into her cheeks. "You did!" He pretended to consider it. "Hmm, on second thought…"

"Oh, just get on with it," she grumbled.

"See what I mean? No patience."

She resolved to frustrate him by showing no reaction to anything he did. He began to unbutton her blouse in an unhurried fashion. Then he spun her back to face the desk and stood behind her. He brought his hands around to cup her breasts and lightly brush her nipples through the fabric of her new bra. She pressed her lips together to keep from making a sound, but she couldn't control her uneven breathing. Her chest rose and fell with the force of it.

"Remember when you were touching me, but I couldn't reciprocate because I was driving?"

She didn't answer, partly because she had decided not to talk to him until he set her free, and partly because she was distracted by him unhooking her bra. This one had a convenient front clasp, making it easy for him to expose her breasts to his touch. He palmed them and now firmly ran his thumbs over the hard nipples.

Kendra stayed quiet as he turned her back toward him and kneeled down before her. His mouth moved all over her breasts, even the undersides, but he saved the nipples for last. He was driving her mad as his tongue lightly circled them. Her clenched mouth failed to hold back a pitiful sound of longing.

He finally licked her nipples, but it wasn't enough pressure. She pushed her chest forward, and he teasingly moved back to deny her the contact that she wanted. Kendra realized what she was doing and sat back against the chair in humiliation. He resumed leisurely licking her nipples as she held herself still.

"That's right. You have to be patient to get what you want."

She looked at him after he spoke and found him watching her intently. He kept his eyes fixed on her face as he opened his mouth to take her nipple into it and begin sucking. The erotic look on his face combined with the intense pleasure after the buildup in anticipation broke her resolve. She moaned in wanton arousal as he finally gave her nipples the attention she had been craving.

After pleasuring her there for what seemed like a long time, he pulled back from her breasts and slid his hands up her thighs. All her attention was now focused on the sensations his touch aroused on her skin. The barely there brush of his fingers over her panties wrenched another moan from her.

Her legs opened wider in encouragement for him to continue. He lifted her flirty skirt out of the way and stood up to walk toward his desk. Kendra's eyes widened when he returned with a pair of scissors in his hand. His other hand slid under the waistband of her panties to lift them away from her skin while he cut them off of her.

"Hey," she protested. "Those cost money."

"I'll buy you more." He dropped the flimsy fabric on the floor and returned the scissors to his desk.

Dominic kneeled before her once more and slid her forward toward the edge of the chair so she was more easily accessible to him. He began to kiss his way up her thighs. His mouth and his tongue explored every part of her nether region that he could reach—except for her neglected clit. He kept finding his way back to it and circling around it, moving torturously close to it before retreating again.

Kendra was making sounds that were a cross between a moan and a whimper. The handcuffs jangled in her desperate attempts to grab his head and place him where she wanted him. He drove her so insane with desire that she was actually forced to beg for it.

"Please, Dominic. Oh, please lick me."

"Lick you where? You have to tell me," he said in a voice so rough that she barely recognized it.

"Please lick my clit," she pleaded.

"I can't hear you," he told her to force her to say it again.

"Lick my clit!" Kendra exclaimed loudly, wincing in shame. She didn't have enough shame not to obey him, however.

He splayed his tongue over her clit but held it there motionless as she squirmed desperately against him.

"Oh," she cried. "Please, oh please lick my clit."

His tongue began to lap at her clit, but it moved at a maddeningly slow pace that wouldn't allow her to have the fast and furious release she wanted. Her moans became embarrassingly loud as his soft, wet tongue brought her climax on by excruciatingly gradual degrees.

After such a slow build, she came very hard. "Fuck yes!" she screamed.

She threw her head back as her body shuddered in ecstasy. Kendra felt the handcuffs loosen from her wrists as Dominic unlocked them. She opened her eyes to look at him.

"Do you know how much you fucking turn me on?" he demanded roughly as he pulled her out of the chair and bent her over the couch much more impatiently than he had the last time.

She had seen by the feral look on his face that he was very near to losing control, and she immediately felt him bury himself inside her. Whether deliberate or not, he was again hitting her G-spot with every thrust. Incredibly, another orgasm began to build within her. She had a moment to marvel at how perfectly his body fit with hers before she was again lost to the sensations of their physical joining.

Kendra decided to take a relaxing bath afterwards. She locked the bathroom door so Dominic couldn't disturb her. "Believe it or not, there are times when you're not wanted."

"That's harsh, Kendra," he said before she closed the door in his face.

"Don't forget to ask for vacation time at work tomorrow," he reminded her as he drove her home.

"I'm not sure if I should let you take me somewhere far away. Who knows what you'll do."

He winked at her. "That's half the fun. What's life without a few adventures?"

She received a package in the mail on Thursday. The small box contained two pairs of panties. The first was a sheer red pair with a slit in the crotch. The second was a white silk pair that looked like they could be bridal lingerie. There was also a note from Dominic.

Dear Kendra,

I like both sides of you. Naughty and nice.

Yours,

Dominic

She stared at that word for a long time, wondering what it meant. Was he really hers?

CHAPTER 21

*E*verything was perfect between them for two months. Kendra lived for the weekends with Dominic. No matter how tiring and stressful her workweek was, she could always count on enjoying the weekend with her boyfriend. She had finally let down her emotional guard enough to view him that way.

Unlike when they were in high school, she could think of what they had as a relationship instead of a fling. She began to relax into it and allow it to become part of her life. Happiness seemed to abound all around her suddenly as Kelly announced her engagement to her boyfriend, and Samantha found a steady boyfriend to replace her penchant for one-night stands.

Dominic appeared to have made a real connection to her this time. It was like having the friendship they had shared before hooking up in high school and the great sex that had come afterwards. He had even showed her the trick to opening the handcuffs. It required the use of a bobby pin to manipulate the lock.

"Want to try?" Dominic offered with a not quite innocent expression.

"No way. You're not going to get me into those things again," she vowed.

"It's not like you didn't enjoy it. And we could take turns being restrained."

A little thrill shot through her at the thought of having him at her mercy. She could think of lots of ways to tease him, but that would entail trying out oral sex on him. That was still making her nervous, so she kept putting it off. Dominic had never mentioned it or even hinted at expecting her to do that for him. He gave her so much pleasure that way, however, that she was starting to feel guilty about not returning the favor.

"You know how to get out of them," she reminded him.

"Not without the bobby pin," he told her.

"Maybe we'll try that again sometime," she replied vaguely.

"Maybe we will," he agreed and dropped the subject.

Even without playing sexy games, things were still hot and heavy between them. He seemed to be able to turn almost anything into a seduction, especially dancing. Maybe it was his new way of teasing her, but he began to prolong their time out in public. After dinner, he would now take her dancing too.

He wouldn't touch her in inappropriate ways, but the tension between them would build as they swayed to the music and looked into each other's eyes. She was very aware of his hands on the small of her back and the sensual movements of his body. He would give her that seductive look before leaning in to speak into her ear as his hand made a slight, gentle caress on her back.

Then, instead of saying something suggestive, he would tell her that she looked lovely tonight or that she was wearing a gorgeous dress. He would then pull back to look at her and smile in his wicked way. Of course, just when she came to expect this from him and stopped reacting to it, he chose to say something dirty to her at a company function.

Kendra had been thrilled when he invited her to go with

him. It was a fancy affair, and she bought a classy new dress for it. Dominic told her that she looked divine, and he was on his best behavior as he introduced her to his coworkers.

He made her feel so special with how much attention he lavished on her. She had expected to stand idly by while he conversed with people she didn't know, but he included her in everything and bragged about her job at such a successful firm. He was the attentive boyfriend, getting her drinks and making sure that she was having a good time. So lulled was she by his perfect, gentlemanly manners, that there wasn't even a hint of the underlying sexual tension that was usually on the back-burner between them just waiting to spring into action the moment they were alone.

They were slow dancing in a pleasant, proper manner when he leaned in to whisper in her ear. "I'm going to drive home with one hand on the wheel and the other on your clit."

Dominic pulled back to see her suddenly flushed face and smiled brightly. "Oh look, there's my boss. Let me introduce you, darling."

He didn't make any more sexual comments before they left the party, but he had planted the seed in Kendra's imagination.

"Did you have fun?" he asked as they walked to his car.

"Yes," she answered. "Thanks for inviting me."

He gave her a disapproving look for thanking him. "Kendra, you're my girlfriend. There should be no question that I would take you with me."

The warm, sappy feeling in her heart made her smile dreamily at him. He leaned in for a sweet kiss before opening the passenger door for her. He got in the car and turned on the ignition before buckling his seatbelt.

Turning to look at her, he said, "Everyone's jealous of me for having such a smart, beautiful girlfriend."

Just as she was melting from his wonderful words, he

changed his tone. "We've been nice all evening. Now it's time to be naughty. Don't you agree?"

"I'm not sure we should," she began.

She was wearing a long dress, but it had a slit on one leg. Dominic ran his hand up the exposed thigh and slipped it under her panties. "You feel sure. Have you been having naughty thoughts, Kendra?"

She gasped in response when his finger brushed over her clit. "You have to drive."

"If I let you drive, we'll crash for sure, because I'd have both hands free and be able to use my mouth too. Do you think you'd be able to pay attention to the road that way?" His finger moved over her clit again.

"No. We should—oh!—we should wait until we get back to your place."

"Okay." He removed his hand from between her legs and put the car in drive. "Just remember that you're the one who suggested waiting to come."

He carefully pulled out of the parking space and began to drive. "Take off your panties," he commanded in a no-nonsense voice.

After a moment's hesitation, Kendra complied. She wiggled around in her seat as she maneuvered the virginal white panties he had bought her off her body and dropped them on the floor at her feet. Then she boldly pulled her dress up to expose herself to him.

He glanced over at her and placed his hand between her legs. "I'm going to watch the road. You need to keep your hands still so I can focus on driving. I'm the only one who's doing the touching until we get back to my place. Do you understand?"

There was something sexy about the way he took control of the situation. She found herself responding to the authority in his voice. "Yes," she answered, her breathing already uneven.

He teased her during the entire drive back, and she liked it.

After the handcuff incident, she felt comfortable enough with him to really let loose with the dirty talk. She knew that it turned him on, so she pleaded with him to make her come.

After a while, the plea was no longer just for his benefit, but she held herself back from grabbing his hand and making him finish the job. Kendra then told him how much she wanted him and what she wanted him to do to her. The F word flew readily from her lips as she craved having him inside her.

Dominic looked as close to losing control as she was by the time he parked the car. It was a tense, silent walk to the elevator. As soon as the lone other person on there with them got out, Dominic stopped it after it began to move again.

"What are you doing?"

She gasped as he dove under her dress and began to suck on her clit. Kendra leaned against the wall and came within seconds. Dominic then stood up and pressed the button to resume the elevator's climb to his floor.

He barely got his apartment door closed before she attacked him. Her hands impatiently freed him from his pants, and he groaned as she stroked him. She sank down to her knees without even thinking about it and took him into her mouth. The strangled sound he made at her surprise move filled her with a heady sense of power. She didn't get very far into her new way of exploring his body before he pulled away from her.

Kendra looked up to see his dark eyes burning into her. "Hmm," she said. "I think I might need to use those handcuffs on you after all."

He pulled her up into a deep kiss that tasted like her, but she found that she didn't mind it.

"No time," he rasped. His hands fumbled with removing her dress before he lifted her up and impaled her against the door. He slammed into her until he came.

It was only when she felt his warm seed spilling inside of her that she realized they'd forgotten to use a condom. "Dominic?"

His breath came in short gasps as he pulled back to look at her with hooded eyes. "Couldn't wait."

He carefully set her down and caught his breath. "Sorry. Just give me a minute, and I'll make you come."

"It's not that," she told him. "We, uh…"

She took a deep breath. "We didn't use anything."

"Fuck," he swore. "I was so wound up that I wasn't thinking."

"I can go buy some emergency contraception," she said. "It can still prevent a pregnancy if you take it within so many hours after sex. Could you go get my overnight bag out of your car? I'll get dressed and drive to the pharmacy."

"Maybe we should wait," he said.

"It's better not to wait. The sooner you take it, the better your chances are of it working." She looked around the floor and then remembered that her panties were also in his car.

Dominic walked up to her and took her hand in his. "I meant that we should wait and see what happens. You might not get pregnant anyway, but I don't want to prevent it if it's going to happen."

She stared at him. "I thought that you didn't want kids."

He smiled ruefully. "I was eighteen. What the hell did I know?"

"We're not even…" Kendra shook her head.

"C'mon, there's something I want to talk to you about." He led her over to the living room couch.

"I got a promotion at work," he continued after they sat down. "I'm moving to New York, and I want you to come with me."

She was stunned by this news. "When?"

"I leave in three weeks," he informed her. "I know that you have three months left on your lease, but after that—"

"How do you know that?" Kendra interrupted him.

"I asked Samantha that first day when I came to your apartment. So, you can tell her tomorrow that you won't be renewing your lease, and that'll give her time to find a new roommate. I'll find us a place you like in New York. We can search together online for what you want."

"Wait." She put a halt to his planning. "Why would you ask her that? We weren't even dating yet."

He gazed at her intently. "I made the mistake of losing you once, and I wasn't going to let it happen again. I didn't want to rush you, but I knew right away that I wanted to be with you. I've never stopped thinking of you in all this time, and I was so happy to see you again. When I called you Miss Davis and nobody contradicted me, I knew that you weren't married. It wasn't too late for us."

"I never stopped thinking about you either," she admitted. She took a shaky breath. "I have a job here, Dominic, and a lot left to pay on my student loan. I can't quit a good job to follow you to New York."

"You hate your job," he said. "I know it pays well, but it's not your dream job. You'll have a chance to get into the field you want in New York. You can apply at the prosecutor's office."

"Who knows when and if I'll get hired. My bills aren't going to be postponed in the meantime," she noted. "I still have to keep making payments on my student loan."

"I'm getting a hefty raise with my promotion, so I'll be able to cover everything. You don't even have to work at all if you don't want to," he told her.

"I'm not going to expect you to support me," she insisted hotly. "I can pay my own way."

"If you're pregnant, you might want to take some time off until after the baby's born." He actually smiled at the thought of it. "There's nothing wrong with staying home for a while."

"Nothing's been decided yet," she cautioned. "Don't act like this is a done deal."

"You don't want to be with me?" Dominic asked.

"I didn't say that. It's just a lot to think about all of a sudden," she explained. "Let's deal with one thing at a time, please. I can't decide my whole life right now."

"Okay," he agreed. "What about the possible pregnancy situation? Will you wait and see what happens?"

It was crazy to take a chance like this when she had an option to prevent it, but she found herself reluctant to interfere in the outcome. His surprisingly enthusiastic reaction to having a baby with her had stirred her own maternal instincts. That didn't stop her from breathing a sigh of relief when she got her period the very next week. Dominic surprised her again when he sounded disappointed by this news.

His tone brightened as he spoke of their upcoming trip. "It's probably for the best. I wouldn't want you to suffer from morning sickness during our first trip to Fiji."

She noted that his words implied there would be more trips to Fiji for them. It was hard for her to reconcile this new Dominic with the one who had broken her heart after high school. Could she really trust in a future with him?

"Did you talk to Samantha yet about the lease?"

"Not yet," she answered. "I was too focused on finding out if I was pregnant or not."

"Now that we know, we can move forward with our plans."

She wasn't as optimistic about things as he seemed to be. What if she changed her whole life for him, and things didn't work out anyway? She was so distraught over her tough decision that she actually confided in Kelly.

"You have a lot more to lose than I did," Kelly said, surprising Kendra with her astute assessment of the situation. "My job wasn't a big deal, but you could make partner here eventually. It'll be hard to replace this job, but I still think you'll have a harder time replacing Dominic."

"Are you kidding me?" Samantha demanded when Kendra explained the situation to her. "You're going to miss out on love because of your pride?"

"I don't want to depend on a man," Kendra insisted. "Also, nobody has said a word about love."

"He's asking you to move in with him. Unless he wants to be your sugar daddy, I'd say he's in love with you. If you're worried about me, don't be. I can always move in with my mom if I need to. She's single now, and she told me that her door is always open for me."

With her coworker and her roommate both urging her to accept Dominic's offer, Kendra called Caroline for advice. She turned out to be no help either, because she was thrilled for Kendra. "I wouldn't have to think twice about it if I were you."

"What happened to the modern woman?" Kendra asked. "What about being independent?"

"You said it would only be temporary until you find another job," Caroline reminded her. "Besides, it's so exciting and romantic! Moving to New York City with your man."

She squealed when Kendra told her about the pregnancy scare. Her best friend was the only one she would tell about something that private.

"What more proof do you need, Kendra? He would have freaked out about the pregnancy if he wasn't in love with you."

Dominic asked her again that weekend if she had talked to Samantha. She told him that her roommate was fine with her moving out at the end of the lease. "That's not really the problem."

Dominic regarded her with the most serious expression she had ever seen on his face. "What *is* the problem?"

"I've worked really hard to get where I am, but the truth is that I got this job because my ex-boyfriend's uncle is a senior partner. He said that he kept me on only because I proved myself as an employee, not because Craig was my boyfriend."

Dominic nodded. "They wouldn't keep a slacker employed, no matter who she was dating."

"I don't want to use guys to succeed. I want to get there on my own merits. I let Craig talk to his uncle about getting me the job because I was desperate, but I never felt right about it," she explained. "I don't want to put myself in the same situation of depending on you for my finances."

"It's only a temporary situation until you find another job," he argued. "I know you're not a user, Kendra. Being together means that we're a team. We pull for each other and give the other person a hand when they need it."

She loved the way he had phrased that, and she fought the urge to succumb and let him take care of everything. "I've made up my mind, Dominic. I'm staying here until I pay off my student loan."

Deep disappointment was plainly visible on his face. "I wish you'd reconsider."

"I'm sorry," she said, her heart breaking. She had tried to prepare herself for the inevitable breakup.

"It's not going to be easy, but I'll fly back as often as I can. You can visit me as much as possible too. We'll have our vacation in Fiji soon, so that'll help."

Kendra looked at him, afraid to believe that he still wanted to be with her. "You're not breaking up with me?"

He was startled by her question. "I already told you. I'll never make that mistake again."

"But you said that long distance relationships don't work."

"I was eighteen at the time. Now I know that I don't want anyone else," he told her. "But is that what you want? Do you want to break up with me?"

"No," she denied fiercely. "No, Dominic. I don't want anyone else but you."

He took her in his arms then and kissed her passionately. They were both so sure, and she tried not to let doubts about their future ruin their time together now.

She was miserable without Dominic. Her life felt ridiculously empty without him, and she chided herself for this less than liberated thinking but was unable to snap out of it. She had always believed that a woman didn't need a man to make her life complete, but she missed Dominic terribly. Talking on the phone just wasn't enough.

With his new promotion, he was busier than ever. Working six days a week didn't allow her any time to visit him either. Thank goodness they had their vacation coming up soon. It was all she could think about lately, and it wasn't for the exotic locale. She just wanted to be with Dominic.

Kendra felt like she was living on autopilot now. She went through the motions of her routine like a robot.

"You're depressed girlfriend."

She had been sitting on the couch staring at nothing when Samantha's voice broke through her mindless preoccupation. "Oh, I was just lost in thought."

"No, you weren't. You were moping. When are you going to stop being stubborn and go be with your man like you want to? You're obviously in love with him."

Was she in love with Dominic? She had wondered about his feelings, but she hadn't given any thought to her own.

Samantha watched the play of emotions on Kendra's face and let out a frustrated sigh. "You're too cautious for your own good. Take a chance on something for once in your life."

"You seem like a modern woman, Samantha. So, why are you telling me to change my life for a man?"

"Because you're not happy with your life. If you loved your job, it would be a different story. If you had anything here to be excited about, I would say don't go. I know I don't see you for most of the day, but I haven't seen you smile once since Dominic left. Can you honestly tell me that you're better off without him?"

"I don't know what to think anymore," Kendra answered.

She had wanted to be strong and independent, but she now wondered if it was worth the price of losing Dominic. No matter what he said about waiting for her, she knew that not being together would prove to be too lonely. He would eventually seek solace in the arms of someone else. What would she have then? A cold, empty life of being married to her job? She couldn't imagine being with anyone else now.

Kendra realized that she must really be in love with Dominic if she felt this way. She began to reconsider her decision, but she didn't say anything to anyone yet.

Then she got the call from him that his mother had died. He sounded terrible on the phone as he related the events of the past week. She hadn't talked to him all week, because he had sent her a text that he had a grueling schedule and would call her after it was over. Kendra had begun to suspect that he was planning to break up with her. Instead, he had been dealing with his mother's death and attending her funeral.

"Why didn't you tell me?" Kendra demanded. "I would have been there with you."

"I didn't think it would be a big deal," he said.

She couldn't believe her ears. "What?"

"I know that's stupid," he admitted. "She was my mother, but we were estranged for so long. I didn't think it would hit me as hard as it did."

"Oh, Dominic. I'm so sorry."

"I never gave her a chance. She tried so many times to talk to me, but I just shut her out. Now it's too late."

She could hear the anguish in his voice, but she couldn't think of anything to say that would comfort him. "How's your dad holding up?"

"Better than me, actually. He says he's just grateful for the time he had with her, and that she didn't have to suffer. She had a heart attack and collapsed in the driveway while they were walking to the car. The ambulance arrived in five minutes, but she was already dead."

His deep sigh made her wish that she was there to hug him. "They think it was the excessive drinking she did for all those years that damaged her heart."

"I always thought that alcohol destroys your liver," she said.

"It can, but it can also weaken your heart muscle. They have a medical term for it, but I can't remember what it's called now. Anyway, they think that's what happened with her."

"That's a shame," she commented sadly. "After she finally got her life straightened out."

"Yeah," he agreed.

She knew that he was regretting not reconciling with his mother. "Listen, Dominic. You had every right to be mad at her."

"I know I did, but I should have had it out with her instead of just giving her the silent treatment. Maybe I wouldn't feel so empty now if I had talked with her, or even screamed and yelled at her. I had a second chance with her, Kendra, and I blew it."

Her heart broke for him. "I want to come see you. Where are you going to be?"

"I'm going to stay with my dad for a few more days, but you don't have to—"

"I'm coming home," she declared. "I'll call you when I get there." She was already logging onto her computer to book a flight.

"Okay," he relented. "I've missed you so much."

"I've missed you too," she told him. "I really don't think that I can take not seeing you anymore."

There was a different tone in his voice when he spoke again. "I feel the same way. Call me back when you know what time you'll arrive. I'll pick you up from the airport."

"You don't have to do that. My parents can pick me up."

"No," he insisted. "I can't wait to see you."

Kendra paid for the flight with her credit card and then called her boss to let him know that she was taking a couple days off.

"Your boyfriend's mother doesn't qualify as family," he said.

"I know sir, but I haven't taken any sick days at all this year. I was hoping that you could overlook it this one time. He's completely devastated by his loss."

"Okay," he agreed. "I'll code you for the sick days this one time, but I can't keep granting you special favors. I appreciate your honesty, however."

"Thank you, sir. I understand, and I have some things to discuss with you when I return." At this point, she had already made her decision, but she wanted to talk to Dominic first.

"Alright, Kendra. We'll talk when you get back."

Dominic picked her up at the airport when she arrived in their hometown. She only had a carry-on bag, so she didn't have to wait by baggage claim. They embraced like they hadn't seen each other for years. She couldn't believe that she had voluntarily denied herself the feeling of having him in her arms.

"I'm so sorry," she exclaimed while she hugged him tight.

"It'll be okay now," he murmured against her hair. "You're here."

He carried her bag as they walked hand in hand to the parking garage. "I know your parents are looking forward to spending some time with you, but can I see you after dinner tonight?"

"Of course," she said. "I came here to be with you. We can stop and see your dad on the way to my parents' house."

"Tomorrow," he promised. "I want you to myself today."

She observed him as he drove, and she was surprised to see that he looked better than she had expected him to. He was even able to smile at her when he glanced over and caught her gazing at him.

Her parents were watching for their arrival, and they came out to offer their condolences to Dominic. Kendra had a pleasant visit with them while they caught up, and they told her funny stories about the grandchildren.

"Boy, Veronica has her hands full," Kendra laughed.

"It's payback for what she did to us," her mom said. "Your children get you back for all the trouble you gave to your parents."

"Then mine will give me no trouble at all," Kendra said. "Because I was the perfect child."

"You must have amnesia then," her dad commented. "That's the only way you could have forgotten the big wheel incident."

"That was Veronica's idea," Kendra told him.

"You were the big sister," he countered.

Her mom shuddered. "You could have both been killed."

The infamous big wheel incident occurred when Kendra was eight and Veronica was six years old. They had been playing in a neighbor's yard, but they were nowhere to be found when their mom came to call them in for lunch.

The other kids thought that they had gone home, but they had instead taken off for the nearby highway on their big wheels. Kendra had been afraid as they approached the entrance ramp, but Veronica had called her chicken. They had blocked up two lanes of traffic as they raced each other down the highway. The police came and returned them to their frantic mother.

Kendra told all these stories to Dominic, hoping to lighten his mood. She realized that they had been driving for a while. "Where are we going?"

"To look at the stars."

He pulled into the same parking lot where they had been all those years ago on their first date. They were dressed casually this time, but the view of the stars was just as magnificent. Dominic put his arm around her as they stood gazing up at the night sky.

"I wanted to come here where it's just the two of us," he said. "Because all I really need is us."

He let go of her and stepped in front of her to drop down on one knee. "I'm asking you to marry me, Kendra."

"Oh my God," she breathed.

"I know the timing is strange, but I don't want to miss out on anymore second chances. I'm going to ask for a transfer back to Chicago when I get back to work."

"You'd do that for me?" Kendra asked in wonder.

"I don't want this promotion if I can't be with you."

"I was planning to give notice at work," she said, laughing through her tears. "Because I wanted to move to New York with you."

He stood up and gently swiped a tear from her cheek. "Why are you crying sweetheart?"

"Because I'm so happy," she exclaimed.

"Does that mean you'll marry me?" His hand tenderly caressed her cheek.

"Yes!" she cried.

He kissed her sweetly beneath the stars. "I love you, Kendra."

Happy tears began to flow again, and she smiled through them. "I love you, Dominic."

As they drove back, she thought how they had come full circle. This was where their relationship had started, and it was where they were making a new beginning now. Change was a good thing, she decided.

"Did she say yes?" Mr. Miller asked as soon as he saw them.

"This is why I couldn't bring you to see my dad earlier," Dominic told her. "I knew he'd spoil my surprise."

"Where's the ring?" Mr. Miller inspected Kendra's hands.

"We haven't gotten it yet. Kendra's going to pick out the one she wants when we go shopping in New York," Dominic informed him.

"What, we don't have jewelry stores here? You can't have your fiancé going back to Chicago without a ring. Her girlfriends will tell her to dump your ass."

Kendra laughed. "He does have a point."

"Okay, okay," Dominic grumbled good-naturedly. "We'll go shopping for a ring tomorrow."

Mr. Miller hugged her. "Welcome to the family, Kendra."

"Thank you." She smiled at him and then sobered. "I'm sorry for the loss of your wife."

"Thank you. I know that she would have been thrilled for you and Dominic."

They went in to announce the news to her parents when he drove her home. They had only just found out that she was dating him again, so they were very surprised.

"Yeah," Kendra told them. "We reconnected in Chicago a few months ago."

"Is he still hot?" Veronica asked on the phone the next day.

"Smoking," Kendra confirmed. "So, will you be my maid of honor?"

"Sure," Veronica agreed. "God, I have to go on a diet. Where's the wedding going to be? New York or Chicago?"

"It's going to be right here, because our parents are here. We're going to live in New York, though."

She had decided to quit her job and apply for that position in the prosecutor's office. It was what she had always wanted to do, and she wouldn't give up until she succeeded. In the meantime, she was going to work at her current job until she left for Fiji. That would be enough time to train someone else to take over her position. She would discuss the details with her boss the following day.

"Gotta go," she said to Veronica. "Dominic's here. We're going shopping for the ring."

"Okay, let me know when you set the date."

Kendra smiled as she hung up the phone. She and Veronica got along much better since they had become adults. Her phone call to Caroline would wait until she got back from her shopping trip with Dominic. She would have to leave him again tomorrow, but this time she knew that it was just temporary. It was fitting that she would begin her new life with him in paradise, because it seemed like her entire relationship with him had been about new experiences and adventures.

CHAPTER 23

Kendra had a moment of sheer panic when she stepped out of the building on her last day of work. What was she doing? She had just walked out on financial security to go live in an unfamiliar city and rely on a man she had only been dating for a few months. The ring on her finger was only a promise, not a guarantee. She felt like going back inside and pleading to keep her job. Her replacement had already been hired, however.

The entire day had been emotional as she said goodbye to her bosses and coworkers. Kelly had even cried, and Kendra had been very close to breaking down herself.

"We're going out to party girlfriend," Samantha announced when Kendra arrived home.

"I have to pack," Kendra said.

"Please, you've been packed for two weeks already. Don't worry. I won't get you into any trouble. There will be no hookups and no hangovers. We're just going to have a fun girls' night out."

"Thanks, but I'm really not in the mood." Kendra sat down wearily on the couch.

"That's why you need this," Samantha insisted. "I can see that you're freaking out."

Kendra didn't deny it. "I didn't think this through."

"You just have cold feet," Samantha told her. "Everything will be fine once you see him again."

She was meeting Dominic at the airport tomorrow, and they were flying to Fiji together. They would stop at the apartment and pick up the rest of her clothes on the return trip. She was leaving behind her furniture, because Dominic had already furnished his apartment in New York.

Kendra suddenly felt like she had nothing but the clothes on her back. She hadn't wanted to stiff Samantha on the rent, so she was paid up for another month even though she was leaving. At least she had somewhere to stay for a little longer if she needed to.

She allowed Samantha to drag her out, because she was driving herself crazy with worry. They had a few drinks, but they spent most of the evening dancing. Kendra loosened up and forgot her troubles for a while.

"Benjamin asked me to move in with him, but I think I'm going to hold off for a while. Play a little hard to get."

Kendra giggled at that.

Samantha laughed. "I don't mean hard to get that way. Just in the doing his laundry kind of way."

"Benjamin," Kendra said. "I never pictured you with a Benjamin."

"Who did you picture me with?" Samantha asked.

"Someone named Spike." Kendra giggled again.

"Ha! You're a little drunk girlfriend. I didn't know you were such a lightweight. You must be a cheap date."

"Hey," Kendra exclaimed. "That's what Dominic said. He was going to get me a happy meal, but I wanted grown up food."

"I'd kick his ass if he wasn't taking you to Fiji," Samantha huffed.

"Yeah Fiji," Kendra sighed. "He had a poster in his room. No girl posters, but he had lots of girls. School player. Yeah, he was. I wanted him so much," she finished with a faraway look on her face.

Samantha tried to make sense of this jumble of sentences. "Wait, when was this?"

"High school." Kendra sighed again. "He dumped me."

"Whoa! Are you saying that you dated him before?" Samantha didn't wait for an answer before continuing. "No wonder you're freaking out."

"He says it's our second chance. Do you think he means it?" Kendra implored her to banish her doubts with the mixture of hope and fear on her face.

"He asked you to marry him. I think he means it," Samantha said.

"Yeah." Kendra looked down at the engagement ring on her hand.

"Okay, now that we've settled that. Let's get back on the dance floor and sweat out that alcohol. You're done drinking for tonight. You've got a plane to catch tomorrow girlfriend, and I'm gonna make sure you're on it."

She was on it, and so was Dominic. He flew in from New York to catch their flight to Fiji. All of her anxiety disappeared the moment she saw him walking toward her. *It's really happening*, she thought. *We're really doing this.*

Samantha hadn't been able to follow her past the security checkpoint, so Kendra was waiting for him alone. He was pulling his carry-on bag behind him, but he let go of it to kiss her just like in a scene from a movie.

"Ready to go to Fiji?" Dominic asked after pulling back to look at her.

"Yes," she agreed, suddenly meaning it. "I'm ready."

Excitement overwhelmed her when they began boarding.

She had never flown first class before, and she chided Dominic for spending so much money.

"It's our first vacation together, so I splurged. Besides, it's a fifteen-hour flight. You'll be glad we got comfortable seats."

He let her sit beside the window. "But this is your dream," she protested. "Don't you want to enjoy the view?"

"I'll definitely be enjoying the view," he teased. "Anyway, you've never been to Fiji either. I can sit beside the window on the trip back."

They settled into their seats and waited for the plane to take off. It was a while before they began taxiing down the runway. Kendra listened to the safety instructions about the emergency exits and using their seat cushions as flotation devices. She tried not to think about them crashing out in the middle of the ocean.

"Ever heard of the mile high club?" Dominic whispered in her ear.

She gave him a disbelieving look, and he laughed. Surely, he was kidding, Kendra thought. There was barely enough room in the tiny bathrooms for one person. "You'd have to have your own private jet for that," she told him.

He grinned. "I'm working on it." He leaned close to her ear again. "I'll hold you to that once I get one."

She whispered something very naughty in his ear and was thrilled to see a slight flush creep over his skin. Kendra suddenly couldn't wait to get to the hotel and have her way with him. They had spoken on the phone, but they hadn't seen each other since their few days together back in their hometown when they got engaged.

Having him beside her in the flesh was so much different than communicating through technology. Something about having that physical contact reassured her in a way mere words couldn't. The look in his eyes as he gazed at her and his brief, comforting touches to her hand or her arm all helped to convey to her the bond they shared. It was strong and intimate, and they would continue to develop it well into the future. Her doubts faded as the plane took them far away from her routine life in Chicago.

Kendra tried not to complain as the hours dragged by. She was going to paradise, so she should be thrilled with this entire trip. Dominic laughed quietly beside her. "Just imagine if we didn't have these comfortable seats. Those poor people in economy are squished like sardines."

"It seems like we've been on this plane forever. How much longer to go?"

He checked his watch. "Seven hours."

"Oh my God," she whined.

He slipped his hand onto her lap beneath the thin airplane blanket. "Do you want me to distract you?"

"No," she said in a shocked whisper and stopped his hand's stealthy journey to the juncture between her legs.

He chuckled softly into her ear. "Lean back and try to get some sleep. I'll wake you when we get there."

Kendra doubted that she would be able to fall asleep in her seat, no matter how comfortable it was. To her surprise, she found herself being gently shaken awake by the flight attendant. Dominic had also fallen asleep, and they were leaning against each other cozily. He stirred when she did and rubbed his eyes sleepily.

"Please lift your seats into the upright position and buckle your seatbelts," the flight attendant told them. "We'll start our descent soon."

Kendra eagerly looked out the window, but all she could see were the fluffy clouds beneath them. She chided herself for taking that glorious sight for granted, but the spectacular view once they got below the clouds thrilled her.

"Look," she cried as she grabbed Dominic's arm and moved her head back so he could see.

They stared out the small window together at the gorgeous

colors of the ocean. The dark blue gave way to the same blue green she'd only seen in pictures. The lush green island was surrounded by nothing else except ocean and sky. It felt like they were at the edge of the world far away from the rest of civilization.

All traces of exhaustion and aggravation at the length of the flight faded from Kendra's mind as they finally arrived at their destination. She waited with growing excitement as Dominic retrieved their luggage from baggage claim.

Their hotel had sent a shuttle to pick them up, and the tourists all gawked out the windows at the natural beauty of the island as they drove away from the airport. Fiji was closer to Australia than America, so there were plenty of Australian visitors. To Kendra, it added to the exotic appeal of the beautiful place.

Dominic had apparently splurged on the hotel too, because it was obviously one of the better hotels on the island. "I guess this will count as our honeymoon," Kendra said as she looked around the fancy lobby while they waited to check in.

"No," he replied. "I'm not going to miss out on another chance to go away somewhere with you."

She wasn't going to argue with that, but she thought she better start looking for a job as soon as she arrived in New York if he was intent on spending money like this.

Their room had an ocean view, but Dominic was more interested in looking at Kendra. "I missed you so much," he said before kissing her passionately.

"Let me take a shower first. I feel icky from all those hours on the plane," she told him.

He ran his hands down her back and over her rear. "No, you don't. You feel just right," he countered in a husky voice, but he stepped back and let her go into the bathroom.

It was stocked with complimentary soap and shampoo, so she didn't bother opening her luggage yet. She didn't need a change of clothes right now, because Dominic would just remove them from her. After their time apart, Kendra wasn't comfortable enough to walk out completely naked, so she stepped into the bedroom with a towel wrapped around her. Dominic's dark eyes still swept over her in appreciation.

"I'll be right back." He went quickly into the bathroom to take his own shower.

Kendra sat down on the bed and waited in excited anticipation. She still had the towel wrapped around her when he emerged naked and aroused from the other room. Her eyes moved from his erection and over his sexy body all the way up to the smoldering lust in his hungry gaze.

The same look must be on her own face, because she was burning with desire for him. She stood up and dropped the towel on the floor in a blatant offering of her nude body to him. He pressed his hard body against her soft curves as he kissed her. She quickly found herself lying on the bed as Dominic buried his head between her legs in his feverish urgency to taste her. Kendra was suddenly toppling over the brink and calling out his name as she shuddered with the intensity of her orgasm. He rose up and reached for the box of condoms he had set out on the nightstand.

"No," she said. "You don't have to. I'm on the Pill."

"For how long?" Dominic asked.

"Since right after we got engaged. It's been long enough to be effective," she explained.

Kendra had made the decision when she was sure that they were in a monogamous relationship. She wanted to enjoy the freedom of having no barriers between them.

Dominic appreciated the fact that she trusted him that much. There was something more than lust in his dark eyes as he gazed at her. "I love you, Kendra."

"I love you, Dominic." The emotion showed in her eyes as

she gazed into his. Then her lips curved into a seductive smile. "Now get in here where you belong."

"A mischievous glint danced in his eyes. "Where?" He slipped a finger into her. "Are you sure I'll fit?" Another finger joined the first one and curled toward her G spot as his thumb played with her clit.

"Dominic," she gasped.

"What?" His fingers rubbed over the sweet spot that no one else had ever touched.

"Now," she pleaded. "I want you."

"Say that again," he ordered as his magic fingers intensified her pleasure.

"I want you," she cried. "Please, Dominic. I want to feel you inside me."

He was too turned on to keep teasing her, so he removed his fingers and positioned himself between her legs. Dominic moaned as he thrust into her, and Kendra grasped his back while he fulfilled her desire. She loved to hear the sexy sounds he made as he approached his climax, and it spurned her on to her own orgasm. They lay spent for a while, luxuriating in having lots of leisure time to relax and do whatever pleased them.

Kendra was the first one to get up off the bed after deciding that she wanted to go to the beach before getting something to eat. Dominic lazily watched her rummage through her luggage and pull out a bikini. She had bought several for the trip, because she had never been to a tropical place before and wanted to indulge. This one was a bright pink color, but she also had a blue one and a red one in her suitcase. Dominic was still sprawled on the bed after she finished putting on her bikini.

"Are you coming?" Kendra asked as she looked in the mirror.

"I'm sure I will." He came up behind her and cupped her breasts.

She could feel his erection pressing into her. "Again?"

"I had all kinds of thoughts about you during that long flight," he murmured against her ear as his fingers caressed her suddenly hard nipples through her bikini top. "Did you have naughty thoughts about me?"

"Not a one," she said breathlessly.

"Liar," he rumbled against her. "You'll pay for that." He yanked her bikini bottom down in a surprise attack, making her gasp.

Kendra spread her legs for him as he reached between them. She leaned back into him and caught his gaze in the mirror. "I'm counting on it."

His wicked smile thrilled her as much as his skillful touch, and she allowed him to see and hear how potent his effect was on her. They spent their vacation enjoying each other and their beautiful surroundings. It was pure bliss being able to make love whenever the mood struck them, day or night, while also partaking of all the natural pleasures that paradise had to offer. They were soon tanned from fun-filled days spent in the sun, and satisfied from restful sleep after heated love-making sessions. Kendra couldn't imagine their honeymoon being any better than this.

"What are you thinking?" Dominic asked as she stood staring pensively out at the blue world of the ocean on the morning of their last day in Fiji.

"I don't want to go back to reality. Life is perfect here with you," she told him.

He wrapped his arms around her waist and pulled her against him. "Life is perfect for me as long as I'm with you. Living in New York was hell without you, but you're coming with me now. I'm looking forward to showing you our new home."

One hand slid downward from her waist. "The bedroom." She hadn't worn panties to bed, so there was no barrier between her bare skin and his hand. "The bathroom, the kitchen, the office."

His fingers played with her teasingly. "I took your favorite couch with me," he rasped into her ear.

"You're insatiable," she said in an unsteady voice.

"Only for you." He turned her around to face him. "We can find paradise anywhere when we're together."

As he took her into his arms, she had to agree that what he said was true. They had started their life together in paradise, but they had already found happiness with each other. This was only one stop on their journey together through life, and it had begun for them way before they set out on this trip.

"I have something to show you when we get to New York," Kendra told him as they packed their luggage that evening. "It's my diary."

"That's funny. I was just thinking about your diary. I never finished editing it, and I think it's about time I did."

"Not that diary pervert," Kendra laughed. "It's my diary from when I first met you."

"Ooh, more secret thoughts." He grinned. "I can't wait to find out what other fantasies you had about me."

"These are romantic ones," she said. "Back before you corrupted me, and I was still sweet."

"Oh, you're still sweet," he said as he advanced on her.

"Dominic," she warned. "We have to finish packing. We've got an early flight tomorrow."

He picked her up and carried her toward the bed. "Yes, and I'll have to control myself during that very long flight. I have to have something to tide me over until we get to New York."

She watched him take off his clothes. "If I kept a diary about this vacation, it would all be X rated."

He started taking off her clothes. "Not all of it. We didn't spend all our time in this room."

She surprised him by pushing him down and straddling him.

"When we weren't in our room, you were whispering in my ear what you were going to do to me when we got back to our room."

"I don't have a diary, so I have to share my thoughts with you when they pop into my head." He reached out to touch her bare breasts.

She moved back out of his reach. "Which head?"

His breath caught in his throat as she maneuvered herself between his legs and leaned over him. "This one?" He felt her warm breath before she took him into her mouth.

He moaned as her head moved up and down his length. Kendra became more and more turned on as she listened to his responses. Dominic stopped her when he couldn't take anymore. He tumbled her onto the mattress and straddled her before thrusting deep inside her. She reveled in the feel of him, and in knowing that she would still be with him after they left Fiji.

They finished packing afterwards and took their showers before going to sleep. Kendra woke in the middle of the night to find Dominic between her legs with his tongue on her clit. "I was trying to sleep," she breathed.

"Oh, sorry." He moved off her and lay back down to sleep on his pillow.

"Dominic," she demanded. "Finish what you started."

He pretended to be asleep, and she shook him. "Dominic!"

The sneaky bastard let out a fake snore. She lay back on her pillow in a huff. "Fine, but I'll get you back."

"I'm counting on it," he said with a soft laugh. "Goodnight, Kendra."

She pretended to be asleep and heard him chuckle again. They got an early start in the morning in order to catch their flight. Kendra let him sit by the window this time, and they both watched the gorgeous view of Fiji until they couldn't see it anymore.

Kendra then whispered into Dominic's ear what she was planning to do to him after they arrived in their apartment in New York. It involved his handcuffs and her teasing him with her mouth. She settled back into her seat and glanced at his lap.

Kendra took the blanket out of the seat pocket in front of her and ripped open the plastic cover. "Here. It looks like you need this." She handed the blanket to Dominic with a smirk.

He covered his lap with the blanket and smirked back at her. "You better get your sleep during the flight."

Kendra was still smiling when she closed her eyes. She was on her way with Dominic beside her, and she couldn't wish for anything more.